I0744954

Hyacinth

CHRIS KENISTON

Indie House Publishing

Indie House Publishing

BOOKS BY CHRIS KENISTON

Hart Land
Heather
Lily
Violet
Iris
Hyacinth
Rose

Farraday Country
Adam
Brooks
Connor
Declan
Ethan
Finn
Grace
Hannah
Ian
Jamison
Keeping Eileen

Aloha Series Heartwarming Edition
Aloha Texas
Almost Paradise
Mai Tai Marriage
Dive Into You
Look of Love
Love by Design
Love Walks In
Flirting with Paradise

Surf's Up Flirts
(Aloha Series Companions)
Shall We Dance
Love on Tap
Head Over Heels
Perfect Match
Just One Kiss
It Had to Be You

**Other Books
By Chris Keniston**

Honeymoon Series
Honeymoon for One
Honeymoon for Three

Family Secrets Novels
Champagne Sisterhood
The Homecoming
Hope's Corner

Original Aloha Series
Waikiki Wedding

ACKNOWLEDGEMENTS

I will freely admit I had a blast writing this story, and I truly hope y'all enjoy reading it even more! A little secret – I named one character after my daughter's kitty so thank you, sweetie, for the inspiration!

Waiting for a new baby in the family is quite the distraction. I have found myself relying more and more on good friends. Once again Dale Mayer came to my rescue sparking the idea for Herman. Kathy Ivan was a lifesaver when it came to writing the short descriptions we call blurbs. Thank you both!

As a person who is allergic to the kitchen, I have to thank dear Mrs. Pohle. Not only for putting up with me in her living room for so many late nights studying or report writing with her daughter, but for being such a marvelous baker. Thank you for the apfel kuchen!

Enjoy!

CHAPTER ONE

Find a nice quiet place, he'd said. Leave the modern world behind, he'd said. You'll get more work done, he'd said. I know the perfect place, retired Marine Colonel Francis Stewart had insisted. At least Alan Stewart's grandfather had been right about something; Lake Lawford was one of the most beautiful and peaceful places he'd ever been to.

Too bad it wasn't doing a dang thing for his productivity. At this point, Alan was so far behind he could see his own shadow. Not even the dummy in the middle of the room was helping. Weaving his fingers together he stretched his arms, the cracking of knuckles filling the air. Now if only the sound of fingers tapping on the keyboard could do the same. Staring at the screen he shook his head. Why was this suddenly so difficult? For almost a month he'd been holed up in this cabin searching for his mojo. Actually, twenty-nine days, fourteen hours and—he glanced at the lower corner of the laptop screen— twenty minutes, but who was counting.

Lifting his hands to his arms to rub away a chill, he turned his attention to the fireplace and the intricate structure of logs and kindling waiting to be lit. Not something folks raised in the south learned to build. For the last month temperatures had fooled everyone into believing summer had come early to New England. Not once had it occurred to him to light a fire. He'd done little more than admire the pile of logs. Until now. Today he wondered if Mother Nature was off her meds again.

Since nothing else was working, pushing his seat away from the small desk, Alan crossed the room, shook his head at poor Harvey taped to the chair, and hunched down in front of the old stone fireplace. Somewhere there had to be matches. It took a few seconds to realize that the lovely foot-long hand-painted box to the right of the carved mantle held the matches he needed. It took another moment to discover that the underside of the box was the strike plate. Maybe he'd buy the cabin owner a lighter gun. Not as pretty, but much more practical. Any man who had ever lit a barbecue knew that.

Only two attempts and gloating in his caveman success, he held the lit stick to the crumpled newspaper stuffed under the logs with the kindling. It took just a moment for the paper to catch. Who said back to nature wasn't easy? Another second and the flames shot up like an erupting volcano. The surprise of it all knocked Alan back on his haunches. Well, flat on his backside, but who was he going to tell?

Shoving upright, he returned to his makeshift desk. Maybe once he warmed up he could get some work done. The snap and crackle of the newly lit fire was like a mesmerizing melody. Already the heat filled the room and warmed his bones. Rubbing his hands together, he laid his fingers on the keys, eager to feel the words come to life.

Unfortunately, the only thing coming to life was the smoke in the chimney. Like tendrils in a horror flick, gray waves filled the room. Now what? Shoving his chair back, he jumped to his feet, bolted across the room, and stared at the smoking fireplace. He should've just raised the thermostat. Vaguely remembering having seen a fire extinguisher under the kitchen sink, he pivoted in that direction and from the corner of his eye spotted a large framed lettering propped prominently on the mantle. *OPEN the flue before starting a fire.* Of course. But who in heaven's name wants to stick their arm up a raging fire to open a flue.

To the right a stand of iron utensils held one potentially helpful piece. Suddenly the crook end of a poker made sense. It had nothing to do with pushing and moving logs, it was all about idiots like him who forgot to open the flue. By the time he located the metal lever and pushed it to the opposite position, he might as well have been standing by San Francisco Bay on a foggy fall day. Even though the fireplace now sucked smoke up the chimney, it did nothing for the blanket of thick air hovering in the tiny cabin's living room.

Freezing cold or not, he had no choice. He opened one window, then the other, and waving his arms madly, threw the front door wide open. All he needed now was for some neighbor to call Hart House and report he'd set the place on fire. Grabbing his notebook and the nearby magazine, he did his best to dissipate the cloud of smoke. So focused on his efforts, he almost missed the big tan streak dashing from the porch through the front door and past his ankles until it almost knocked him over and darted down the narrow hall. Quickly, panic licked at his racing heart. What the heck was that? He'd spent more than one afternoon sitting on the front porch and had yet to see anything approach the cabin. He'd spotted a couple of deer up the hillside in the trees, but none of them had been young.

Though now that he thought about it, wasn't spring the time for all new critters? Could it have been a baby deer that flew past him? Wouldn't he look silly calling Animal Control over a baby fawn. Shaking his head, he quickly closed the windows. No point giving another animal easy access. On his way down the hall, he hesitated a moment by the kitchen to grab a broom. Just in case. The only open door led to his bedroom, a space too small for anything to hide. Actually, he expected to find the scared and nervous fawn huddling in a corner. When the room looked completely untouched, that meant one thing: whatever had come inside was under the bed.

Sucking in a deep breath, he reminded himself this was not a television show or a horror flick, or even a Stephen King novel. His imagination was probably worse than whatever was actually hiding under the bed. Not standing too close, he got down on all fours and carefully tilted his head into the dark space. His first concern should have been the rumbling growl that vibrated under the low mattress. He was pretty sure fawns didn't growl. Glowing green eyes met his. He had absolutely no idea what animal had green eyes and growled, but by the time his brain registered the snarling teeth, he was up and out of that room faster than a speeding bullet. Imagination be damned.

At least he was proud of himself for two things. One, not getting mauled to death. And two, having kept his wits about him enough to close the door behind him. Searching for his phone somewhere on the tabletop, his mind ran through a list of the most likely angry critters that could roam the nearby woods. Mountain lion—okay, maybe a bobcat—kept jumping to the top of the list. Neither of which he could see Fiona Hart or George the handyman grappling with. Like it or not, he needed serious help.

• • • •

"Well, top of the morning to you." Katie O'Leary smiled up at Cindy as she came around the corner, arms laden with several loaves of the shop owner's famed Irish soda bread.

"And the rest of the day to you," Cindy answered. As kids, the traditional Irish response had been a joke. As an adult, she savored any opportunity to be transported to a gentler, kinder place and time. Any chance to spend time with Katie O'Leary did that. Even though the woman had been born on this mountain, raised by her Irish grandmother, she had enough of the Emerald Isle in her to be a breath of fresh air to anyone who crossed her path.

"Looks like you're feeding an army."

Cindy laughed. "Not quite. Lucy asked me to come by and pick up a few things. The General has had a hankering for her corned beef, and since the grocery store had a big sale on point end corned beef, Lucy saw no reason not to accommodate him."

"And a good job of accommodating the entire family she does."

"Absolutely." Cindy could not argue. Lucy was technically her grandparents' housekeeper and cook, but as far as the grandchildren were concerned, she was family. There wasn't a thing any of them would not do for Lucy, and she was pretty sure there was not a thing Lucy wouldn't do for them. Though most of them wished that Lucy would stick to cooking and cleaning, and bypass the Dolly Levi matchmaking.

"Has Lucy had any luck in getting that young hermit out of his cabin?"

Cindy shook her head. "The man doesn't open his door for anyone. The few times he's asked for room service, he's told Lucy to have George leave it on the porch."

"I'm wondering if maybe the man has an embarrassment to hide. You know, a nose like Cyrano de Bergerac, or a chin like the Wicked Witch of the West."

"Or a mask like the Phantom of the Opera?" Cindy smiled.

Katie shook her head. "Now I won't be making anything that dramatic. But the man must have a strong reason to keep to himself for this long. He hasn't come into town for anything. This time, I'm thinking Lucy may be right. It may be time for some of us folks to make an extra effort to bring the man out of his shell."

"Out of his shell?" Cindy narrowed her gaze, interpreting the simple comment and hoping it did not mean Lucy was up to her old tricks.

"Now don't you look at me like that. I'm not the one who wants your sister Poppy to start making the deliveries to the cabin instead of George."

She knew it. Heaving out a sigh, Cindy supposed she should be grateful that Lucy wasn't planning on locking her sister in the cabin with the man, or poisoning his food so that someone would have to stay and care for him. Or was she?

"And what has your face suddenly looking like you sucked on a lemon?" Katie asked, placing the loaves of fresh bread in a cardboard box along with some of the other items Cindy had picked up.

"Nothing." Lucy wouldn't stoop that low. After all, as much as folks teased her about setting the house on fire, she didn't actually set it on fire. Cindy shook her head. Now she was just being silly. Placing a few more items in a second box, she looked up at the smiling shopkeeper. "I think this is it."

"Excellent. Let me help you to the car." Katie came around the counter.

Cindy waved her off. Placing one box on her hip, she reached for the other box with her free arm. "They don't weigh much. I can do this."

"Of course you can. And I suppose you're going to open the doors with your teeth?" Chuckling at her, Katie grabbed the second box and started for the exit.

"Thank you." Cindy walked out the door that Katie held, her gaze spotting a big old red fox darting across the road at the same time a car sped out of the neighboring road. Cindy's heart lurched in her throat. Yakking with the person in the passenger's seat, the driver obviously did not see the animal in its path.

"What is it, dear?" Katie came to stand beside her, quickly observing the same thing. "Oh, dear."

As sure as her name was Hyacinth Nelson, DVM, the car knocked the poor animal halfway across the road and kept going. "Damn it." Practically dropping the box, she hurried to the curb waiting to see if the fox would shake it off and get up or if he was more seriously injured. When the animal remained lifeless in the middle of the road, she shook her head.

Katie had no doubt been waiting for the same thing. "I've got some blankets in the back. I'll go get them. If he's not out cold you're going to need something to help trap him."

Nodding, Cindy ran to her vehicle and pulled out her veterinary bag. This was another reason why the mountain desperately needed its own wildlife center for rescue and rehabilitation. Her small clinic was full up and too understaffed to keep a full-time eye on an injured fox. Hurrying across the road, and hoping the little guy would just wake up and run off before she got there, a small pup waddled out from under a bush to stand beside his hurt parent. *Double blast.* Since fathers and mothers both parented their pups, she couldn't see from this distance which parent had been hit, but if the snarling little one had his way, she wasn't going to get close enough to find out.

Heels clacking rapidly on the pavement, Katie appeared beside her, holding a pet carrier in one hand and blankets in the other. "Oh my. Where there is one, there has to be more."

"That's exactly what I was thinking." Cindy looked around for signs of more pups, but so far this was the only one. "Now all I have to do is get close enough without having that little one snap at me."

Katie nodded. "I'll take care of that."

Shooting her arm out to stop the woman from hurrying any closer to the injured animal, Cindy shook her head. "The last thing I need on top of an injured wild animal is to have you hurt as well."

"Nonsense, that little fella's teeth won't do any damage."

Cindy tried really hard not to roll her eyes. When it came to any wild animal, even a fox, it wasn't just the bite she worried about. Any disease the animals carried, including rabies, could pose a much bigger problem. "Let me see how close I can get."

"Lass," Katie touched her arm, "I know you have a way with the animals, but there are two of them and two of us. Let's do this together."

As much as Cindy did not want to risk Katie getting hurt, she knew the woman was right. She also knew the woman had a way with people and animals alike. She just hoped this was one of those times when Katie's special way would work its magic.

Slowly inching toward the two animals, and hoping no clueless driver would come barreling up the road, Cindy crouched, speaking softly to the still snarling and snapping pup beside its dead or unconscious parent. "Easy fella. No one is going to hurt you."

Stepping around her, Katie softly moved ahead, smiling at the pup. She didn't say a word. She merely sat down just outside of snapping distance, opened the blanket on her lap, made a ticking sound with her throat, and much to Cindy's surprise, the little guy stopped snarling.

"Okay. Maybe I need to hire you to work at the clinic." Heaven knew, Cindy and her techs had been snapped, bitten, and scratched by more four legged creatures than she cared to admit.

Not wanting to interrupt the connection between Katie and the pup now tilting its head and studying the shopkeeper, Cindy debated how close she dared get to the injured fox. In the next second, the decision was made for her. Without hesitation, the furry guy walked straight into Katie's lap and curled into a fluffy ball.

"No maybe." Cindy chuckled. "I definitely need to hire you for the clinic."

Wrapping the ends of the small blanket around the baby fox, Katie ignored the compliment. "Now you can check on the mama."

Turning her head, Cindy got a better look at the injured fox. She was indeed the mama. And thankfully, she was still alive. Now all she had to do was get the girl to the clinic and pray she could fix her up in time to reunite her with the rest of the pups.

CHAPTER TWO

"""S o what's the verdict?" Katie asked.

Of all the possible worse case scenarios Cindy could think of, this was most definitely not one of them. The x-rays were clean as a whistle. "Looks like the dislocated joint is her only problem. Possibly mild concussion. When she wakes up from the meds I gave her all she'll be is a little sore. I'd like to observe her overnight, but tomorrow I'll take her back to find the rest of her family."

Katie nodded. The woman, God bless her, had insisted on closing the One Stop in order to help Cindy transport the animals and keep the little guy calm.

The mama fox had only been stunned. Lethargic and eyes glazed, she'd started to come to just as Cindy had given her a tranquilizer. Unlike humans that a doctor would want to keep alert to determine injuries, veterinarians did not have that luxury with wild animals. In this case, she was pretty sure it was all going to work out for everyone.

"Good. I'll keep my eyes open. And when you're ready to let mama out, I'll be there to help."

In her pocket, Cindy's cell vibrated. The sheriff's office. She tapped speaker phone. "Hello?"

"Hi Doc, it's Nadine. Sorry to bother you so late in the day, but since this call that came in is out on your family's property, and the sheriff would just have to call you anyhow, I decided to cut to the chase."

A lot of things could be said about Nadine, but getting to the point was rarely one of them. Cindy couldn't fathom what would be happening on her grandfather's property that would require her or the county police. "What have you got for me?"

"One of the cabins, Aspen, says they have a mountain lion trapped inside."

"They said what?"

Nadine chuckled. "Yeah, that's what the guy said. He must not know there aren't any mountain lions this far northeast, but something's growling under the bed and if it is a bobcat, you'll need to tranquilize it to take him or her back where it belongs."

"Got it." The Aspen cabin was where the hermit had been hiding out. According to the little information her grandfather had shared, he was from someplace down south or west. She had no idea if the man knew his bobcats from his mountain lions, or any other dangerous animal, but Nadine was right. Any trapped animal could be very dangerous. "I'm on my way."

"Sounds like you're having a busy day," Katie said.

"Ain't that the truth. I'll drop you off on my way."

"And then when you're done you can tell us if we've got Cyrano de Bergerac or the Phantom of the Opera staying at the cabin."

Cindy smiled. If the guy wanted her to get whatever was trapped inside out, he'd have to let her in. "Will do."

It didn't take long to drop Katie off at the One Stop and wind her way around to the most isolated cabin on Hart Land property. This guy definitely must like communing with nature. Unlike the other cabins, there was little chance of running into another guest or a family member unless you went out of your way to do so.

The place was completely quiet. If she didn't know there was someone inside, she certainly couldn't tell from looking at the place. Windows and doors closed, the thin trail of smoke from the chimney was the only sign of life. Taking a few extra minutes, she walked around the cabin looking for tracks that would imply anything bigger than a chipmunk had moved its way into the house. For a short while she pondered if this guy would know the difference between a possum, a skunk, and a bobcat if they stood in a police lineup.

On the front porch, she looked inside one window, peering through the slit in the curtains. The place did not look like it had been torn up by a trapped animal. The table was covered in papers, plates, drinking glasses, and an open laptop. She moved to the other end of the porch, stopping at the first window with another opening in the curtains. The living room looked fine. Except for one thing. Blinking twice, she rubbed the dirt away from the glass. What had she stumbled into? From behind, she could not tell if it was a man or a woman, but someone was tied to a chair. And she'd bet her last dollar no bobcat or mountain lion had done that.

Cell phone in hand, she quickly snapped a picture of what was inside and immediately sent it off to Nadine with a quick text: *Better send the sheriff and the EMTs. I'm looking for signs of anyone else.* Tiptoeing softly around to the other side, she searched for a window with a view to the inside, but nothing.

Her phone buzzed, and she knew it had to be Nadine. *Look my ass. Get out! Cavalry is on its way.* For once, she would agree with Nadine. Lying low until backup arrived was not a bad idea.

"May I help you?" A deep voice wafted over her shoulder.

Her heart stammered and she damn near peed her pants. Slowly she spun around. With the sun at his back, she couldn't see the face that went with the tall silhouette. The only thing stopping her from freaking out was knowing that any second help would be here. "I, uh. I'm, ah, here about the trapped animal."

"It's under the bed, but you can't go in there."

Any other circumstance and she would've stood straight up, stared him in the eye, and said the hell I can't. But at the moment she merely held up her veterinary bag and wished this mountain weren't so big.

It didn't take long for the guy to put the pieces together. "You're Animal Control?"

She shook her head. "I'm the vet. The police called me." The police? For the first time since stumbling across the victim inside, it dawned on her if this guy were guilty why would he call in the police? "Is this your cabin?"

"Sort of. I rent it. But I am the idiot who let the wild animal inside." Not the answer she would've expected from a mass murderer or kidnapper, or all-around crazy person. "I guess you want to go inside?"

Did she? Now that she'd had time to think things through, something was not adding up.

Not waiting for her to answer, the guy spun about and walked around the corner. Something else that didn't add up. If he wanted another victim, why would he turn his back on her? None of this made sense, but as long as she had backup coming, she might as well find out what the heck was going on.

• • • •

He didn't have a problem with the female veterinarian. He didn't have a problem with a female anything, but this woman looked ready to jump out of her own skin. Not exactly the personality type he would expect to treat sick and injured animals, and certainly not what he'd expect the police to send to deal with a wild animal. He also did not understand why in heaven's name she'd gone snooping around the house instead of just knocking on the door.

Even though he'd known whatever animal he'd trapped in the bedroom would not be able to open the door, he'd felt better waiting for help outside. Though he'd stayed close enough to spot when someone arrived, the brief walk around had done wonders to calm his pounding heart. Now, pushing the front door open, he wished he hadn't been in such a hurry to escape. At least not without taking a minute to put Harvey in the closet. Not that he couldn't explain why Harvey was strapped to the chair, he just didn't want to. Whether in the Northeast, the Southeast, the Midwest, or wherever, small towns were small towns. Maybe if he stood just right, he could block her view long enough to hide Harvey. "It's in the bedroom straight down the hall."

Almost stuck at the threshold, the veterinarian looked down the hall to the table on her left, then at him blocking her view of the small living area, then back down the hall again. Slowly, she took a step inside, and rather then moving straight for the trapped animal, she intentionally looked around his shoulder, straight at Harvey.

"He's a project."

Though she stared at the dummy, her stone-faced expression was not what he had expected. Then again, she was a veterinarian, in the middle of the woods. Perhaps finding a life-size dummy strapped to a chair wasn't the oddest thing she'd ever run into. And what did that say about life being stranger than fiction.

"The animal is that way." He pointed again down the hall.

She nodded, and pulled out her phone. "I need to make an

important call, hang on."

He had no idea what was suddenly more important than a wild animal trapped in his bedroom, but hang on he would.

Turning her back to him, she mumbled into the phone. All he could make out was every other word. "Fine... I'm sure... No, that won't be necessary... Yes, I'm sorry... I will... I promise... I know, Nadine... Okay."

"Is everything all right?"

"Yes. I suppose it is." Pulling a flashlight and what looked like a small handgun out of her bag, she marched down the hall.

As unsettling as having his temporary home invaded by a wild animal had been, he hoped that wasn't an ordinary pistol. While he didn't want the animal in his home, oddly, he didn't want it hurt either. "You will be careful, won't you?"

Slowly she looked over her shoulder at him. "Yes."

Torn between his grandfather's code of chivalry and self-preservation, he very slowly followed behind her. While every survival instinct wanted him to retreat to the outdoors again, he would never again be able to face his grandfather if he let that woman go in after the animal alone. Not that he would be much help, even if he had once again snatched hold of the broom.

Inching the door open only a sliver, the veterinarian peeked into the room and listened. Silence greeted her and he wondered if somehow the animal had gotten out. She edged the door open wider, and holding the weapon straight out in one hand, crouched low to the ground and turned on the flashlight.

A heavy sigh filled the room. Putting the gun and flashlight aside, she pushed to her feet and strode quickly to the bed, shaking her head. It didn't take a genius to interpret her frustration to mean he did not have a lion or a bobcat hiding in his room.

On her knees again by the nightstand, she reached into her pocket, and pulling her hand out, held it palm open in front of her. "Come on, Sophia."

Sophia?

She shook her hand, and a large furry head eased its way out from under the bedframe and sniffed at the contents. Once again, he was torn between grabbing her away from the large creature about to bite her hand off and hurry them to safety, and storming forth to do battle with whatever body was attached to that big head.

"That's a good kitty," the woman cooed, petting the furry head. Once the treats in her hand were gone, she wrapped her fingers under its shoulders and pulled the never-ending animal out from under its hiding place.

"What is that?" Half his brain shouted *that's a cat, you idiot*, the other half shouted *Monster*.

"Sophia belongs to Thelma Carson. Though I'm not sure what she's doing this far from home."

"What is this cat on? Steroids?"

The vet shook her head. "Sophia's a Maine Coon."

He'd read enough to know that was a cat breed, but somewhere he must've missed the chapters that said the cat was the size of a large lion cub. And obviously, more friendly, because he could hear the thing purring halfway across the room.

"I'd better get Sophia back to Thelma." Hefting the cat higher on her shoulder the way a mother might carry a toddler child, she pointed to the flashlight and gun. "Would you mind putting those in my bag for me, please."

"Sure." On closer inspection, he could see the pistol was some sort of tranquilizer but handled it carefully nonetheless. Bag in hand, he waved toward the front of the cabin. "I'll follow you out."

The short distance from the bedroom to the porch, she didn't say a word. Not until the animal was secured in an empty crate in the back of her vehicle did she turn and face him. "Thanks for your help."

Not that he'd done much. "Any time." His gaze followed her as she walked around the vehicle and climbed into the front seat. With all the chaos, not till now had he taken note of the easy stride that came from long, lean legs.

Nor the bright blue eyes that twinkled at him. "Also, you should probably put your *project* away. Some people might get the wrong idea." The car door slammed shut and she backed out and drove off down the dirt road.

He didn't know about the wrong idea, but right now he had plenty of ideas bouncing around. Too bad none of them had anything to do with his project.

CHAPTER THREE

"Well, my my." Thelma retrieved Sophia from the carrier. "What are you doing with the doc?"

"I wouldn't mind knowing the answer to that myself." Cindy reached out to scratch behind the cat's ear.

Thelma looked at her wide-eyed. "You don't know?"

"Well, I know how I got custody of Mr. Sophia. What I don't know is how Mr. Sophia wound up under the bed at the Aspen cabin."

Thelma's already rounded eyes circled wider. "Isn't that the cabin with the stranger who won't see anybody?"

"That would be the one."

"Oh my." Thelma put her cat on the ground and turned, grabbing Cindy by the arm and dragged her inside. "You have to tell me everything."

She might as well. Pretty soon the entire town was going to know she'd been on a run to rescue a cat and would be bombarded with questions. At least this way, Thelma would tell Louise who would tell Betty at the Cut and Curl as well as half the town and within five minutes of her leaving Thelma's house, the entire mountain would know whatever she knew. "There isn't much to tell." Quickly she ran through the phone call that led her out to the cabin, skipped over the part about peeking through the windows, or how the man had scared her half to death when he came up behind her while she was peering through the dirty glass.

"Did you see him?" Barely able to contain her enthusiasm, anyone would think Thelma was a six-year-old asking her closest friend if she'd seen Santa come down the chimney.

"I did." She sank into the nearest chair. "And I'm sorry to disappoint, but he does not look like Cyrano or the Phantom."

Thelma's shoulders deflated as she dropped into a nearby chair. "Hmm. Is he really short? You know, like on the TV shows?"

"No—"

"Tall? Really tall?" Thelma cut her off again.

"No—"

Thelma's face scrunched in thought. "Not tall, not short. Does he need a piano case to be buried in?"

"No." Where did Thelma come up with this stuff? Cindy held up her hand to stop the next barrage of questions. "He's just an average man. Probably his mid-thirties. A little on the tall side but not much more than 6 foot. Average weight. Brown hair. Brown eyes. No wooden leg, no hunchback, no eye patch. Just an average guy." She wasn't going to tell one of the Merry Widows that in a Clark Kent sort of way, this average looking guy was actually quite handsome.

"Then why won't he see anybody? He doesn't open the door for Katie when she delivers groceries. He doesn't open the door when Lucy sends up a cooked meal."

"Maybe he wants to be left alone." With his *project*.

"Unless he's Greta Garbo, no one wants to be that alone for an entire month." Thelma tipped her head to one side. "What aren't you telling me?"

"Well," she hesitated, "you might say he's eccentric."

"As in crazy?" Thelma shifted her head left and right. "You know, you could use a little crazy in your life."

"Me?"

"Well, of all your sisters, you are the most serious. I suppose it may have something to do with having to deal with life-and-death more than most. Actually, that makes a lot of sense, since your cousin Heather was the most serious of the whole bunch of you until she fell in love with Jake. Yes," Thelma nodded her head, "you could use a little crazy in your life."

"Now you sound like Lucy." Besides, nobody needed *that* kind of crazy.

"I like Lucy."

"So do I," Cindy agreed vehemently, "but we don't need any matchmaking. I can find my own man. And if I were to pick one, it most certainly would not be one with his..." She paused. "Little oddity."

Staring at her, Thelma's brows rose high on her for head. "How little?"

Cindy really didn't like contributing to the gossip mill, but then again if the man didn't want his business to be known, he shouldn't call the police and leave his *project* out in the open for anyone to find. And on top of that, if she didn't want Lucy and the others playing matchmaker, she needed to lay all the cards out on the table. "He plays with dummies."

"Oh. Well." Thelma leaned back, disappointment taking over her face. "Don't we all?"

"No. I don't mean that kind of dummy. I mean the life-sized kind."

Disappointment shifted to obvious confusion. "What other kind of dummies are there?" All of a sudden, Thelma's eyes flew open wide. "You don't mean the inflatable kind?"

"Close enough. This one wasn't inflatable but from a distance it looked like a real person." Real enough that she'd alerted the police to a non-existent crime.

"You know, I saw a movie once about that. This man was in love with a mannequin. Boy was his sister surprised to find out she wasn't real."

"I'm not sure love has anything to do with this." Fetish maybe. Neurotic possibly. Psychotic very probably. As a matter of fact, she should talk to the General about this character's background. She and Sophia may have gotten out alive, but that didn't mean he wasn't still a threat to the community.

Thelma waved her hand. "I can see the wheels turning. Share."

Odds were, Nadine the dispatcher had already shared Cindy's text alert. "The dummy was tied to a chair."

Silence loomed as Thelma considered Cindy's words. "Do you think he's into M&Ms?"

It was all Cindy could do not to laugh. And she certainly had no intention of explaining the difference between M&Ms and BDSM to a woman who played cards almost nightly with Cindy's grandmother. "Maybe."

Thelma slapped her hands together, rubbing vigorously. "Ooh, this could be interesting."

Mr. Sophia came walking around Thelma's chair and flicking his tail high in the air, leaned into Cindy's leg and then walked away.

"See, even Sophia agrees. We could have a live one."

Cindy looked down at the cat. The animal had spent more time with the man than anybody else. Or at least in his cabin. Wouldn't it be nice if Sophia could tell Cindy exactly what that man was up to?

• • • •

"I still say the root of the problem is that you're not spending any time in the community."

Phone in his hand, speakerphone on, Alan paced the now empty living room. No point in keeping Harvey out in the open for another person to stumble upon. "I thought the whole idea was to get away from interruptions and distractions so my muse would talk to me again."

"There is such a thing as too much silence. Maybe your muse needs to be tickled by a different stimulus."

Alan paused and stared at his phone. "What on earth are you talking about?"

"Sometimes, in the military, we need to think outside the box. And sometimes, in order to accomplish that, we need to immerse ourselves in something outside the ordinary, the routine. You've tried a month of hibernating like a bear in winter. Maybe it's time to go out and face the world. Find an interesting character to spark an idea. Small towns are filled with them. Floyd the Barber isn't even named Floyd."

"Unless Floyd the Barber has a past buried in his garden, I don't think getting a haircut or a shave is going to solve my problem."

"How will you know until you try?"

Funny, that was pretty much the same thing his grandfather had said to him when he talked him into getting on an airplane and flying thousands of miles away from his condo in order to break the mental block. That hadn't made much of a difference; what could giving the old man's advice another shot hurt? "I'll think about it."

"When is your new deadline?"

"All right." Alan sighed. Point taken. He was running out of time. "If my muse isn't talking to me by the weekend, maybe I'll go into town for lunch or shopping or something."

"That's my boy."

Alan smothered a chuckle. He wondered if his grandfather would ever stop referring to him as his boy. A heavy hand pounded on his front door, startling him out of his amusement. He hadn't ordered any food, so he couldn't imagine who would be on his porch. Besides, neither the lady from the One Stop nor anyone from Hart House knocked with that much…vigor. "I don't suppose you've sent somebody to visit?"

"What?" The old man's voice dripped with sincerity.

"Never mind. I need to answer the door. I'll keep you posted."

"Sounds good. Love you."

"You too," he bounced back, jumping when the heavy hand pounded again. "Coming."

Rather than glance through the window to satisfy his curiosity, before the man could bang again, Alan drew the door open wide.

Like a scene from one of his books, the country Sheriff stood, his back to the sun, mirrored glasses reflecting Alan's surprise, and he was pretty sure the officer was scowling at him.

"May I help you?" That was probably the stupidest thing Alan had ever said, but he wasn't sure what else to say when confronted with a frowning lawman for no reason. At least he hoped it was for no reason.

"May I come in?"

Did innocent people actually say no? He stepped back. "Of course."

The sheriff scanned the entire contents of the room in one long glance. "I understand you had some trouble today?"

Relief washed over him. This was about the cat. "Yes. Turned out to be a neighbor's Maine Coon."

Whipping off his glasses, the sheriff glared at him under furrowed brows. "Maine Coon?"

"Yes. The cat. That is why you're here?"

The sheriff took two steps further into the room, once again scanning from left to right and back. "Mind if I have a look around?"

Oh, Alan really did not like the sound of that. "Of course not."

Slipping his glasses into his pocket, the sheriff gave a curt nod and began walking the small space. He'd taken his time in the bedroom, opened the closet, checked behind the shower curtain, and returned to the living room. "I understand you've been here almost a month?"

Alan nodded.

"You plan on being here much longer?"

So much for small-town hospitality. "I'm not sure."

The sheriff scanned the cabin once again as if expecting to find something the last two scans had missed. "What is it you do here all day?"

"Work."

"At what?" The man fished his glasses out of his pocket and slid them back onto the bridge of his nose.

"I'm a writer."

The sheriff's glance landed on his laptop. "What kind of writer?"

"Murder mysteries."

"I see." Removing his glasses, he nodded. "And what would this particular book you're working on be about?"

Some days, Alan was a little slow on the uptake. And today was definitely one of those days. This was about Harvey, happily tucked away in his trunk. "A serial killer. Recently I've been working through a difficult section. It's hard to find new ways to tell a story where a victim is held hostage or captive. I sometimes use props to help me work out a scene."

The sheriff paused, considered Alan's words, then nodded again. "As long as you stick to your props, we shouldn't have any problem."

This time Alan nodded, thankful he wasn't about to write his book from the inside of the county jail. "Yes, sir."

The lawman walked out of the cabin to his patrol car in a few long strides. Climbing into his car, he pulled the door shut and rolled down the window. "You might do both of us a favor."

He nodded. Again, did people actually say no? "What would that be?"

"Be extra careful not to scare my citizens with your props." The man smiled and drove away.

An image of a stone-faced veterinarian studying Harvey came to mind. A beautiful stone-faced veterinarian. Too bad he'd probably already scared one citizen permanently away.

CHAPTER FOUR

Weaving his fingers and stretching his arms out, Alan cracked his knuckles. The sun had been up for little more than an hour, and except for the few minutes it had taken to put on a pot of coffee, he had spent most of that time typing.

From the second his feet had hit the floor this morning, scenes had begun to form in his mind. Despite staring at Harvey tied for over a week to the chair in the middle of the living room, by the time Alan had had his first sip of coffee, he'd known exactly where his mistake had been and how to fix it. Now re-reading the scene, he felt the tug of satisfaction in his cheeks. He'd nailed it.

His coffee now cold, he pushed away from his laptop and crossed the small area to the kitchen. The question at hand was what to write next. Pouring the dark brew into his mug, he thought through where the story might go. Too many of the ideas that came to mind, he'd already done. It was almost as if his subconscious was playing a worn out list of his bestsellers.

The sweet aroma of strong coffee teased his nostrils. He could do this. His mojo was hopefully making a comeback. Perhaps a little bit more slowly than he'd like. At least the solid 60 minutes of typing had been more work than he'd managed to accomplish in a very long time. Blowing across the top of the hot liquid, he paused at the table and his laptop. First thing this morning he'd been itching to get at those keys, now he was back to needing a little more time to figure out his character's next move. Maybe another walk outside would get his brain cells firing again.

Standing at the front door, he opted to finish his coffee in one of the oversized rockers that graced either side of the porch. From here he could see down hill to the crops of trees and occasional cabin. The large white Victorian that centered the property peeked up at him through budding tree leaves. Off in the distance, Lake Lawford could be seen shimmering under the morning sunlight. A picture suddenly came to mind. Small boat, family boat, probably a rowboat. A lone figure seated, staring at the rising sun. Slowly, the frail figure pushed to his feet, leaned forward and hefted a large heavy item over the side. Jumping to his feet, Alan ran inside and grabbed one of his notebooks, the one that he normally kept for stray ideas that would come out of the blue. Reaching a fresh page, he scribbled down the scene. Once upon a time he had carried a notebook with him everywhere. This past year, his imagination had taken such a long vacation that he'd forgotten more often than not to keep a notepad at his side. If this morning's inspirations were any indication, he would need to remember to keep paper handy once again. He liked that idea. A lot.

Pushing off the floor, he set the rocker in motion. An odd squeak accompanied the normal creak of the old wooden floorboards. He stopped moving and listened. Nothing. Once again, he set the rocker in motion, sipping his coffee. The normal rhythmic groaning of the floor resumed, followed by the odd squeak once again. This time when he stopped his chair, he could still hear the squeak. Standing, he did his best to hone in on the origins of the odd sound. Coming from his left, he moved slowly in that direction. When he reached the front steps, he spotted the source. Struggling to make its way up the first step was a tiny mewling fuzzball.

"What have we here?" Setting his mug on the rail, he squatted and reached out to scoop up the tiny creature. "You look awfully young to be out on your own."

Snuggling the kitten against his chest, he descended the remaining steps, listening for siblings. He didn't hear a thing out of the ordinary. What he didn't understand was, even if there was only one kitten, why wasn't the mama nearby? He wasn't much of an animal man, but this fellow looked awfully small to be out in the world on his own.

"I think we're going to have to call somebody." His first thought had been to call local Animal Control as he had done yesterday, but his second thought kicked in quickly. "I know exactly who to phone for help."

Cradling the kitten in one arm, he pulled his cell out of his pocket, only two bars, but thankfully it worked. Using his thumb, he scrolled through looking for the veterinarian's number. It dawned on him that in their brief exchange yesterday, he hadn't learned her name. Good thing there was only one veterinarian in the town of Lawford. Hyacinth Nelson. He liked the sound of that. Tapping the number, he waited for the phone to ring

"Veterinary clinic."

It shouldn't have surprised him that the sweet voice on the other end was not the sweet voice he'd been hoping to hear. "Dr. Nelson please?"

"May I ask who's calling?"

He grinned. It didn't matter what he said, neither the receptionist nor the doctor were going to know who he was. "Alan."

Hesitation hung in the silence. "One moment please."

Thank you, Grandpa. Writing was a solitary career. One that did not require he spend much time on the phone with anybody other than his editor or agent. Still, Alan had often used his grandfather's advice when it came to social norms. High on grandpa's facts of life list was function on a first name only basis and people will assume you're a friend. *Mission accomplished.*

"Dr. Nelson." The voice on the other end made him smile.

"Good morning. This is your favorite cat whisperer calling." Silence hung heavily. Perhaps joking wasn't the best start to the conversation. "Actually, this is Alan from the Aspen cabin."

"Ah, yes. Anymore mountain lions hiding under the bed?" Apparently she did have a sense of humor.

"Not exactly."

"I'm not sure I want to know what you mean by not exactly."

"We do have another cat, but this one is not hiding under the bed. He, or she, climbed up the front steps."

"Sophia is back?"

He shook his head even though she couldn't see. "No. Perhaps one of her kittens."

"Not likely. Sophia's full name is Mr. Sophia."

There had to be an interesting story behind that. "Either way, I have a little fellow here who could probably use the attention of someone who knows considerably more about cats than I do."

"Is he the only kitten?"

"Looks like it."

"What about the mom?"

"I haven't a clue."

A deep sigh sounded through the line. "All right. I have to run to the One Stop today. If I can't come and get the kitten myself, I'll find somebody to come pick it up."

He didn't like that idea all. "I could bring him to you."

"I'd hate to make you have to go that far out of your way."

"I have an order in at the One Stop. Instead of having it delivered, I could pick it up and meet you there."

"That could work." Her tone sounded less stressed. "Let me have your number and I'll ring you when I'm on my way."

"Sounds like a plan." He shot off his number and agreeing to meet in a little while, disconnected the call and slipped the phone into his back pocket.

Petting the squirming kitten, he glanced down the road in the direction of the One Stop. Bringing the doctor's pretty smile to mind, he turned his gaze back to the kitten. "I owe you, my young man, or lady, a nice very big bowl of cream."

● ● ● ●

So far today was not going at all the way Cindy had intended. First thing this morning some fool had picked up his aunt from the airport with her dog, putting the dog and the luggage in the back of the pickup truck, and then proceeded to get into an accident halfway home. Of course the poor dog went flying and thankfully this time, Cindy was able to put him back together. Her only consolation had been watching the devastated aunt scold her clueless nephew nonstop. At least Cindy knew the pup would get good post-op care.

In hopes of locating Mr. Fox and the other pups, she had really wanted to take Mrs. Fox and company back to the One Stop before the day got busy. As it was, now she had to add an abandoned kitten to her schedule. "I'm going to put the foxes in the back of my car. If anybody needs me, unless it's an emergency, I don't expect to be back for a while."

"Do you think you'll find the rest of her family?" the tech asked.

"I honestly don't know. But I can always hope."

"Oh, I almost forgot." The tech handed her a flyer. "Nadine dropped this off while you were in surgery. She wants to make sure you like it before she posts them all over town."

Cindy looked at the paper promoting the street fair the town had planned in an effort to support her goal of a wildlife center. It certainly would have come in handy had Mrs. Fox and son needed more extensive rehab. Heck, even an overnight stay would have been easier in a facility designed for wild animals versus her small clinic. Slipping the page into her bag, she smiled at the new tech. "I'll look at it more closely later, thanks."

Tapping in the number yesterday's crazy man had given her, she alerted him that she was on her way. ETA about ten minutes.

In the back of her car, Mrs. Fox was clearly restless. Poor thing probably had no idea what to make of being in a cage for almost 24 hours. Cindy wasn't sure that having at least one of her pups was doing anything to help comfort the sore animal. "Don't you worry, mama. You can go find the rest of your pups in a few minutes."

She pulled into the parking lot by the One Stop. Leaning against his car, ankles crossed, the stranger already waited for her. She had hoped to get at least a few minutes to let the fox out before having to deal with Alan and the kitten. Putting her car in park, she stepped out of the vehicle.

"Good morning, Dr. Nelson." Straightening to his full height, Alan smiled at her.

She didn't think she'd seen him smile yesterday. If she had, she would have remembered it was a nice one. Actually, now that she wasn't concerned that she had stumbled onto a serial killer, she noticed that had she met this man under any other circumstances, it would have been unlikely she'd have described him as average. "You might as well call me Cindy. Everyone does."

He nodded and smiled even wider. "Cindy it is."

"Did you bring the kitten?"

"Yes. He fell asleep playing in a small box and is still snoozing in my car."

She smiled at that. Cats and their boxes. "Good. That'll give me a few minutes to deal with my current patient and then we can take a look at yours."

"Ah, you're here already." Katie O'Leary came strolling out the glass door. "This morning I thought I heard a little commotion out back, but by the time I got there I didn't see any critters."

Had anybody else mentioned commotion or critters, Cindy would not have paid much attention, but Katie always seemed to be hyper aware of her surroundings. "What kind of commotion?"

Katie smiled up at her. "Attagirl. I made it a point to put some scraps out by the trash. I kept an eye on it for a good 30 minutes and nothing. As soon as I went inside to answer the phone, you know I heard scratching and rustling and the sound of the old metal cans bouncing back and forth."

"It would be nice if it was Mr. Fox and family."

"We'll have to see." Katie waved her arms. "Could have been Mr. Raccoon and family for all I know."

That it could've been. There were plenty of deer, raccoons, foxes, squirrels, and four-legged animals willing to rummage through trash in these parts of the woods to fill multiple rescue and rehab centers. Nodding at her friend, she opened the hatch of her SUV. "Are you ready, mama?"

"What have you got here?" Alan asked.

"I have a mama fox that I need to return to the wild." Cindy scanned both sides of the road and either side of the One Stop, searching for the best location to set her patients free.

"Where are you thinking to let them out?" Katie asked.

Cindy turned to face the One Stop. "Maybe behind your place. It looked like mom was going from this side of the street across the road. She could have been moving them to a new den."

"But you think papa is still on this side of the road?" Katie glanced behind her building. "We might as well give it a shot."

Cindy eased the smaller carrier out of the vehicle and handed it to Katie. "I separated mama and son for transportation. Thought it would be easier if we let them out one at a time rather than tried to coax them both out of one crate."

"Sounds like a plan," Katie agreed.

"Need some help?" Alan reached for the larger carrier at the same moment Cindy turned to grab it.

The unexpected contact momentarily startled her. The word nice came to mind once again. Something about this strange crazy man didn't add up. "Thanks, but I've got it."

Reluctance in his eyes, he slowly stepped back. "May I at least come with you?"

She hesitated a moment. Too many people would only make mama more nervous and papa harder to find, but the tenderness in his eyes had her nodding yes. "Stay behind us, don't move quickly, and try not to make any noise."

Alan nodded, and much to her surprise, followed instructions very well. Considering how much bigger than her he was, his steps landed more softly and silently.

"This should be a good spot, don't you think?" Katie's steps slowed, and she pointed to a thatch of shrubbery not far from the building and trash cans.

"Looks as good as any." Cindy bent down and unlatched the smaller crate.

"Since I'm here, you might as well let me." Without hesitation, Katie reached in and slid the little fellow out into the open. She gave him a smooth rub across the back of his head. "You be a good boy and take care of your mama," she murmured before setting him on the ground.

Turning her attention to the larger carrier, Cindy said a silent prayer and unhinged the door. If necessary, she had cat food in her pocket, but was hopeful mama would simply follow her kid. Mama fox stood sniffing the air, and Cindy held her breath. Another moment passed, and mama finally moved away from the crate and nudged her kid.

Softly, Katie murmured instructions. "Go on, mama."

The fox actually turned to look at Katie. If Cindy were a betting woman, she'd have wagered the farm that mama nodded back at her. None of the adults moved, their gazes frozen on the large set of shrubs mama and son had run behind.

Cindy carefully scanned the surrounding thicket.

"Look!" Whispering, Katie pointed to a large tree several yards away.

It took a few seconds for Cindy to spot the nose peeking out from behind the trunk. Another few seconds and she could see more of an adult fox inching forward. She actually crossed her fingers, waiting to determine if this was just any fox.

Alan's hand landed softly on her shoulder, and his warm breath brushed her cheek, accompanied by the soft whisper of his voice. "Is there going to be trouble?"

"I hope not," she whispered back.

His hand remained on her shoulder as the three of them continued to watch the fox dart behind another clump of weeds. Only this time, Cindy's heart gave a kick. In the clump of weeds, she could see another pup. At the same moment Alan's fingers tightened against her skin, she saw what he must have. Mama fox and son had met up with Mr. Fox and three other kids halfway between the trash cans and the tree. Mama licked each of the three pups, and Mr. Fox nuzzled his head against mama's neck.

"Now isn't that the nicest thing you've ever seen?" Katie said on a sigh.

"I think it just might be," Alan agreed, taking a step back, his hand drawing away.

A cool chill replaced the heat where his hand had been. "Yes," Cindy said. "Very nice."

CHAPTER FIVE

"**L**et's have a look at that kitten."

Right. Kitten. So engrossed in the scene unfolding in front of him, he'd almost forgotten about this morning's visitor.

Both Cindy and Katie followed in his wake. He'd left all the windows open for fresh air. Not that heat was a concern this time of year. Hitting the fob, he unlocked the car and opened the door.

"Oh, this is a week for babies, isn't it?" Katie reached into the box and scooped up the little gray tabby. "And where did you get this fellow?"

"I didn't get him anywhere. He found me."

"Oh really?" Katie nuzzled her cheek against the warm kitten. "So he picked you, did he?"

"Not me. My porch."

Frowning, Cindy reached out to take the kitten from Katie's hands. "He's younger than I thought."

"Does look to be about four maybe five weeks?" Katie kept her gaze on the kitten.

Cindy nodded. "I'm afraid so."

He didn't quite get why the two women looked so concerned. "Is that a problem?"

"Depends how you look at it." Cindy straightened her back and handed the kitten over to Alan. "At this age the mother has not usually weaned the kittens yet."

As little as he knew about cats, he already knew he didn't like where this conversation might be going.

"The kitten is probably old enough to start introducing real food. Around this age their curiosity will start poking at mama's dry food, and mama will start nudging them away when they go to nurse."

"This little one is going to need some looking after," Katie said.

Alan looked down at the kitten and attempted to hand it off to

Cindy again.

"Nope." The veterinarian shook her head. "I have a new tech and am short personnel. There's too much going on at my clinic. I do not have time to care for a small kitten. I'm afraid, Mr……" Her words hung.

"Peterson," he provided.

"I'm afraid, Mr. Peterson, this kitten is all yours."

Panic slithered up his spine. He could almost taste the fear he put some of his characters through. "Oh, no."

"Oh, yes." Cindy grinned up at him.

"On that note, if you two will excuse me. I have a business to attend to." Katie took a step back and waved a finger at him. "I'll have your order complete in a minute. The butcher just delivered a rib roast big enough to feed an army."

"What about you?" Alan extended his hands in the direction of the nice Irish lady. "You seem to have a way with animals."

"That I do, sir. But I think you missed the part about I have a business to run. You look quite capable of taking care of that little one. He's all yours." Katie spun around and waved over her shoulder as she trotted back inside the One Stop.

This was so not good. "I don't know the first thing about caring for a baby anything."

"If it makes you feel any better, it's much easier than a baby human."

He shook his head. "No, that does not make me feel better. Not that I have had much contact with baby humans."

"Nieces, nephews, baby cousins?"

"Nope." He shook his head again. "Military brat. I'm the only one in my family who followed a different career path. Everyone is scattered around the country. By the time I get a chance to meet my sibling's children, they are way past that afraid-I'll-break-them stage."

"I don't think we have to worry about you breaking the kitten." She took a step toward the One Stop. "I'll even foot the bill for the supplies you will need."

Feet rooted to the floor, he tried shaking his head again more vehemently. "I don't have time to take care of a kitten either."

Cindy marched ahead, clearly expecting him to follow.

"I mean," he held the kitten tightly against him and hurried after her, "I have work to do."

"Consider him one of your projects." Cindy shoved the glass door open then froze in place and turned to look at him. "Scratch that. I'll show you everything you need. He only has to be fed three or four times a day. You'll probably have plenty of time to do whatever it is you need to do."

"But that's three or four times too many." Grabbing the door with his free hand, he followed her inside.

"I've already started gathering what he'll need." Katie placed a bag of litter next to what he feared was a growing stack of supplies.

"No." He shook his hand at her. "Not me. Someone else needs to do this."

Cindy quickly scanned the items. "Looks good. Better give him a little bit of wet food in case this guy's too young for the dry food mixture."

"Got it." Katie nodded.

"No, we don't *got it*." He tried again. "There has to be somebody else who will know if the cat is too young for wet or dry food because it's not going to be me."

Katie added a couple of cans onto the pile and looked up at Cindy. "Is this going on the clinic tab?"

"Yes." She sighed. "The nearest shelter is overcrowded with kittens already."

"There's a shelter?" Why hadn't anybody mentioned that before?

Katie rolled her eyes. "It's over an hour away. And they have more animals than they can handle. You can do this."

"You seem to have a lot more faith in me than I do." Which made absolutely no sense since she'd sent the sheriff snooping after him. "I have no business taking care of a baby anything. I was traumatized when my goldfish that I won at the state fair died. Trust me, this is not a good idea."

Cindy waved him off. "Everybody's goldfish dies. Let's get you the initial set up. And I'll pop by later and see if we can find mama."

"Okay." Katie slapped her hands together and rubbed with more enthusiasm than the situation warranted. "I'll put this on your tab."

If there was one thing Alan had learned from a military family, it was how to recognize a losing battle. "No. Go ahead and put it on my tab."

The matching grins that took over Katie and Cindy's faces were almost enough to have him volunteering to take on some of the shelter's excess kittens. Looking down on the tiny fur ball that had once again fallen asleep in his hands, he considered his grandfather's earlier suggestion to get more involved. Helping the pretty veterinarian search for mama cat should count for involved, and could prove to be the most interesting thing he'd done in a very long while.

• • • •

"Don't you look like something the cat dragged in?"

Sinking onto the nearest stool, Cindy watched Lucy pull her lasagna out of the oven. "Man, that smells good."

"Your mama popped in earlier. She spoke with your Aunt Marissa while she was here. Seems Iris and Eric and the kids are having a great time in Florida."

"Hope they're not thinking of moving there." Cindy might not have seen her cousin Iris often, but at least New York had been a drivable distance in a pinch and deep down, everyone was hoping they'd settle permanently in Lawford.

"Nope, but your mom seemed awfully tired."

"She's working too hard."

Lucy heaved out a heavy sigh. "I know. That's why I thought since we're not having a roast, I'd make her favorite."

"She'll like that." Cindy smiled. Sometimes she wished at least one of them had gone into the family business so her mom wouldn't have to work so hard at the funeral parlor.

"I heard you had an interesting day yesterday." Her sister Poppy bounced into the room. Her ponytail swishing behind her and her smile brightening the room, she slowed to give Cindy a quick hug. "All anybody could talk about all day was you storming in on a stranger to save the man from a mountain lion."

Lucy shook her head and laughed. "No, no. She saved our guest from a serial killer."

"I thought the guest was the serial killer?" Grams strolled into the kitchen, arms laden with bundles of fabric, her usual smile brightened the room.

"According to Thelma," Lily stood by the sink slicing apples and chuckling, "you saved Mr. Sophia from a serial killer."

"Hardy har har." All of the riotous renditions were actually considerably closer to the truth than some of the stories that had come through her clinic this afternoon. Betty from the Cut and Curl came in to ask how Cindy had single-handedly captured a band of terrorists. And Mabel from the diner thought Cindy deserved a medal for stopping a sex trafficking ring. She wondered how long it would take to get around that all she'd saved was a nice crazy man from a scared cat. Though she still hadn't decided what to make of the dummy in the chair. For some reason, something about this guy kept her brushing that little oddity aside. It just didn't seem to fit with the smiling face that had agreed to tend to a kitten he really didn't want to take care of. She really didn't get it.

"Ooh, apples." Poppy crossed the kitchen and took in the array of ingredients surrounding her sister. "Pie or Kuchen?"

"Kuchen." Lily reached for the flower sifter.

"Oh, that will hit the spot." Cindy had no idea how many generations back they had to hunt in order to uncover the originator of the German *apfel* cake recipe, but right now Cindy was very happy it was on the menu for dessert. Maybe as a peace offering and thank you, she'd take a piece to Alan when she stopped by later to look for the mama cat.

"So." Her Grams set the stack of fabric on the nearby kitchen table and strode over to Cindy's side, giving her a light peck on the cheek and a comforting pat on the shoulder. "What actually happened? The General insists the town has gone mad, that Alan is a perfectly normal young man."

"Katie agrees with the General." Using a spatula to cut her lasagna, Lucy waved it at no one in particular. "She met him this morning over an abandoned kitten and says despite his hermit tendencies and his reluctance to care for the animal, he was actually very nice. Though it's his fault we're not having rib roast for dinner tonight."

Grams cast a curious glance at Lucy. "How is it his fault?"

"He placed an order for rib roast before I did. There wasn't enough left for us. So we're having lasagna. Though lord only knows what a man who hasn't cooked in a month needs twenty pounds of rib roast for."

Cindy felt a pinch between her brows. What *did* he need that much raw meat for? One more thing about the stranger that didn't quite add up. "Maybe it's a west coast thing?"

"Who cares?" Poppy tried to pinch a piece of lasagna from the tray. "I love anything Italian."

Smashing butter, Lily looked up at her sister and laughed. "Especially if it's a cannoli."

Cindy laughed too. They all had a weakness for Lily's cannolis. "You got that straight."

"Katie says that you are going to see Alan to follow up on that kitten." Lucy placed a few large slices of the lasagna onto a heavy-duty paper plate.

Cindy nodded. "I'm hoping I can find the mama and some other kittens. It doesn't make sense there's only one."

"Maybe the stray who has made herself at home under the willow cabin would consider adopting her." Grams sorted the piles of fabric. "One of the guests caught her moving her kittens. As soon as they are weaned, we'll find good homes for them and have the stray fixed."

"I swear," Lucy shook her head, "there's a sign out there somewhere that's telling all wayward mama kitties that suckers live at the big white house."

"And they'd be right." Grams chuckled.

Lucy rolled her eyes and smiled at the woman who had been her employer for as long as Cindy could remember, and handed Cindy a foil covered plate. "I was going to ask Poppy to take this over to Alan, but since you're going anyway would you mind taking it?"

According to the clock on the wall, the family would be sitting down for dinner in about twenty minutes. Not enough time to find a mama cat and be back.

"Lucy," Grams said, "why don't you put an extra slice in and Cindy can join Mr. Peterson for dinner? After the chaos of the last couple of days, he'd probably appreciate the company. Especially if he's nervous about caring for a young kitten."

"Excellent idea," Lucy smiled, "which is why I already added an extra piece."

Grams smiled and laughed. Cindy decided there was no point going against both women. Pushing to stand, she retrieved the plated dinner and waved to her sisters. "Just make sure somebody saves me a piece of *Apfel kuchen*."

She wasn't sure if Thelma and Lucy were somehow plotting to set her up with the nice crazy guy or not. Usually, when Lucy was into matchmaking mode her tactics were not as simple and straightforward as take this man food. Her ideas usually included a threat to life, limb, or sanity. On the other hand, Thelma had come right out and said a little crazy in Cindy's life could be good for her. She shook her head. The fact that Lucy had asked her to deliver dinner to their guest instead of her sister Poppy had to be something as simple as convenience. But just in case, she was going to keep her eyes open.

Since she'd told Alan that she wouldn't be by until later this evening, she'd taken a few seconds before leaving the house to call and let him know she was coming. When he didn't answer the phone, she'd considered waiting until after she'd had dinner with the family to deliver the lasagna, but since both her grandmother and Lucy wanted him to have the food earlier rather than later, she figured if he wasn't home, she could just leave it on the kitchen counter and check on the kitten while she was there.

Having put the car in park, she leaned over and retrieved the aluminum foil covered plate. To confirm her Grams had been right and it was getting late in the day, her stomach growled at the delicious aroma of Lucy's baked lasagna. Alan was in for a treat. As she walked from the car to the front door she slowed her pace, looking for any signs of more kittens or a mama cat rustling in the nearby shrubbery. Nothing.

From the porch, she saw no signs of movement outside or inside. Maybe Alan had gone for a walk? Or could he be taking a nap? Maybe she should've stuck with her first thought and stayed for supper at Hart House until he returned her call. Too late now. She was already here, food in hand. Knocking lightly in case he was resting, she waited a minute, then put her ear to the door. If he was napping, he must've fallen asleep during some old movie. A horror movie. One that played eerie background music.

After yesterday's incident, the hairs on the back of her neck stood straight up. Her new dilemma: stay or go. She looked over her shoulder to her car, then in front of her at the door. She was being silly. Yes, the man obviously had some weird fetish, but she'd been perfectly safe yesterday afternoon and this morning, and just because he liked horror movies didn't mean she couldn't leave him a hot dinner. Gripping the knob, she heaved the door slowly open.

In the same box on the table by his laptop, the kitten was sprawled out flat on its back sound asleep. Stepping quietly inside, she closed the door behind her and with no sign of Alan anywhere in the living area, and the kitten happily sleeping, she opted to leave dinner in the fridge and head back to Hart House.

Rounding the corner into the kitchen, a bright light reflected in her face, stopping her short. What the heck? Blinking, she stepped aside and focused on the shiny object ahead. A knife. A sharp knife. Held high in the air. In Alan's hand. *Holy hell.*

CHAPTER SIX

A shrill scream nearly pierced Alan's eardrum. Following through, he lunged the knife between two ribs as he spotted a stunned Cindy backing out of the cabin. "Wait! I can explain." Grabbing a dry rag from the counter, he tore off after her.

Cindy didn't say a word. Her heel backed against the wooden threshold, tripping her onto the porch. Still holding onto whatever she held in her hands, she whipped around and darted down the stairs.

For a small cabin, it took him nearly as long to get to the porch as it took her to fly down the stairs and fling her car door open.

"I'm a mystery writer," he shouted. He stood very still, hands at his side, hoping she'd heard and believed him. "I'm not a psychopath. I write books."

His repeated declaration must have registered in some way. One leg in the car, her other leg remaining firmly on the ground, she slowly turned to face him.

"Cross my heart." He drew an X across his breast shirt pocket. "It's all for my books. Harvey, the roast, it helps with the details."

He supposed Cindy's silence was a good thing. Though he'd rather have words, at least she wasn't speeding down the hill yet.

Keeping one foot in the car she twisted to better face him. "Harvey?"

"The dummy." He smiled. "I named him after the rabbit."

Her head fell back against the seat and she barked out a laugh. "You named your project after Jimmy Stewart's invisible rabbit?"

He shrugged. "What can I say, I'm an old movie buff."

"Which explains the creepy music." She twisted further back around, setting both feet on the ground.

Letting out a relieved breath, he dared to take a step in her direction. "That's more for mood music. After all, it's the music in Psycho that gets the blood flowing more than the shower curtain, or even the knife."

"Maybe." She hefted her shoulder in an unconvinced shrug and pushed to her feet. "But your books won't have music."

"No." He took another step forward. "But the words on the page, if I do it right, will convey the creepy music for the reader."

She blew out a long slow sigh. "I hope you know that I'm pretty sure I've sprouted several new gray hairs."

"I'm terribly sorry. May I treat you to a nice dinner out and a good bottle of wine as compensation?"

She held up an aluminum foil clad item. "I come bearing Lucy's lasagna."

"In that case, any chance I can convince you to join me for lasagna? I think there's some wine in the cupboard."

"Sounds good." She handed him the dish. "I may need a glass or two before we break bread together."

Leading the way back up the stairs, he smiled. "That can be arranged."

Thankful she'd believed him, and wasn't now reporting to the sheriff that a psychopath was stabbing raw beef in one of her grandfather's cabins, he took a couple of long deep breaths. Even though the evening had taken a turn for the better, his heart still raced like a thoroughbred at the finish line.

"How hungry are you?" he asked.

On the sofa with the now wide awake fur ball, Cindy dangled a toy mouse in front of the kitten. "Half an hour ago I would've said starving."

"And now?" He handed her a glass of red wine.

"Unless you're famished, I'm in no hurry."

"No hurry." He took a seat on the opposite end of the sofa, leaving the kitten playing between them. "He's an interesting creature."

Not lifting her head, she gazed up at him through thick long lashes. "How so?"

"One minute he's jumping and bouncing, attacking that stuffed toy, and the next second, he's asleep on top of it."

Cindy chuckled; it was a nice sound. He liked it. A lot. Certainly more than the scared look in her eyes from a few minutes ago. "They do that often at this age. I have pictures of kittens asleep in their food, their water, or half in and out of the box. They really are adorable."

"He is kind of cute."

"Have you thought of a name for him?"

"Oh, no you don't." He smiled "I'm only helping out. I can't keep him. When my deadline comes, I'm getting on an airplane and going back to San Diego."

She bobbed her head and continued to taunt the kitten with the gray toy.

"Do you really think there are more kittens out there?"

"Hard to say. This may be the only survivor."

That thought left him surprisingly unsettled. In the afternoon he'd spent with this little guy, he'd grown to like him. He didn't want to think of what might've happened to the rest of the litter.

"I do, however," she let go of the toy and looked up at him, "believe somewhere out there, there's a mama."

"Makes sense." He set his wineglass on the coffee table. "Shall we take a walk about and see what we find?"

"Good idea. But let's start with under the house."

"Under the house?"

"Cats aren't stupid." She shrugged. "Roof over their heads, protection from the winds, safety from predators."

He nodded. "Got it. I'll get the flashlight."

Of all the things Alan had thought he might be doing this evening with Cindy, crawling on the ground on all fours had not been anywhere on his radar.

"Any sign of a cat or kittens?" she asked.

"No." He eased out from under the side access, brushed the dirt from his knees, and stood. "Honestly, I don't see anything under there that looks like a nest or signs of an animal circling and creating a sleeping spot."

Surveying the area around the house, she shook her head. "Doesn't make any sense. Kittens don't just fall out of the sky."

"Didn't you say that the mama fox was moving her pup from one den to another yesterday?"

"I did."

"Do cats do the same thing?"

She nodded. "They do."

"As much as I hate to say this, could it be that mama was moving him from one place to another and something happened to her before she moved the rest of the kittens?"

"I suppose anything is possible. But I'd hate to think that there are more orphaned kittens, only without someone to watch over them."

He didn't like that idea either. "All right, let's walk."

Without a word, she fell in step beside him. Taking their time, they looked for ditches under trees and shrubs that might have been excavated by a mama cat protecting her kittens. They also poked at fallen trees looking for hollow logs that might have been made into a home for a litter. Squirrels, chipmunks, and a few other furry neighbors scurried out of the way of their search, but no signs of any felines.

Turning the corner, Cindy came to a full stop.

Nothing around her looked to be a sign of more cats. "Do you see something?"

"Only that." She pointed straight ahead. "No matter how old I get, the sunset over the lake always takes my breath away."

In his month stay, this was the first time he'd even noticed the sunset.

She whirled around to face him. "Don't you agree?"

"Now that you mention it." He took a good long look. "It is rather spectacular."

Her eyes opened wide. "You're kidding right?"

"Nope." He shook his head.

"You've been here an entire month and are only noticing the view now that I mention it?"

"I noticed it. Sort of."

"Sort of?"

"I'm sorry. I came here to work. I spent pretty much all day and night in the cabin staring at a typewriter."

"Or playing with Harvey?" she teased.

"Touché." Taking a second to breathe in the fresh evening air, he closed his eyes and listened to the silence.

"I don't know how my cousins can live in New York and Boston. I'd shrivel up and die if I had to be surrounded by that much concrete."

"There's much to be said for the conveniences that come with all that concrete." Though he lived in the coastal suburbs and not a major metropolitan city, he certainly appreciated the conveniences not available in a small community like Lawford. Coming up for air in the middle of the night after being lost in a manuscript and having twenty-four hour access to food, drink, gas or anything else he might need was a positive for him.

He took in the shades of red, yellow and orange dancing on the water in the distance. This wasn't the first time he'd noticed the lake at the bottom of the hill, but it was the first time he'd stopped to not only really look, but appreciate nature's painting. Twenty-four hour supermarkets didn't seem to matter right now. He had a feeling by the time he finished this book, a lot more than his view of the lake would be shifting.

• • • •

Cindy didn't get it. How could anybody be surrounded by this much beauty and stay locked indoors. Probably why the guy lived in a major hub and didn't bother coming out of the cabin to breathe in the fresh air. For all she knew he was one of those people who broke into hives or something when cut off from technology, or easy access to a major freeway. Though she did need to cut the man some slack. After all, his career dictated he have a desk job. And he wouldn't be the only one who spent too much time locked indoors. The medical world had concluded that sitting was the new smoking. Too much time in a chair, in front of a computer, was slowly killing people.

"I'd say we've done the best we can for now." Alan scanned the darkening area one more time.

"Agreed." Wherever mama kitty was, Cindy hoped Mother Nature was looking out for her.

With the brisk evening air settling in quickly, Cindy found herself hurrying to the cabin. Both of them briefly stomped the dirt off their shoes on the welcome mat and pushed the front door open. It did Cindy's heart good to notice the first thing Alan looked for was the kitten. They'd see who was going home with who by the time he finished his book.

"He did it again." Alan stood at the table. "I have no idea why we bought him a bed. This stupid box seems to be his favorite spot."

Cindy laughed. "Surely you've seen all those Internet graphics showing cats contorted into boxes a fraction of their size."

"I suppose I've seen a few." Shaking his head, he turned toward the kitchen. "Would you like another glass of wine?"

"No, thank you." She followed them into the compact kitchen. "The second dish has some of my sister Lily's bread."

Alan stopped mid-uncovering the dish and turned to face her. "The Pastry Stop Lily? That bread?"

"Yes," she chuckled, "that bread. And to think my sister thought that she didn't have anything special enough to attract enough clientele to stay in business."

"You're kidding me?" Alan slid the lasagna into the oven. "I haven't been into town myself yet, but anything Lucy has sent over made by the bakery has been superb."

"Thankfully, you and a whole lot of people agree. Already Lily has full time counter help *and* an apprentice baker. And it's a good thing too. I have no idea how she'd bake for the shop, bake for the family, and plan for a wedding to beat all weddings next month if she didn't have at least some help." While Alan sliced the baguette, she pulled plates and silverware from the cabinets. "We're all so happy for her. Proud of her. That bakery was her dream since she wore out her first Easy-Bake Oven."

Alan carried the butter dish and sliced bread over to the table. "What about you? Did you dream of being a veterinarian since you were a little girl?"

"Absolutely." She set a couple of placemats down. "If I'd had my way, Hart Land would have been over run with animals."

"So your dream has also come true?"

She forced a smile. "Mostly."

Back in the kitchen, he popped his head out the doorway. "Only mostly?"

"Oh, don't get me wrong. I love what I do. Having my own clinic, taking care of sick and hurt animals, making them well again. That *is* a dream come true. There's just more to the dream."

Oven mitts in hand, he pulled the warmed lasagna out of the oven and carried it to the table. "How much more?"

She reached into her pocket and pulled out the paper she had been carrying around all day. "This would make the whole package."

Unfolding the page she'd handed to him, Alan read the flyer and lifted his gaze to her. "Wildlife Center."

"There isn't anything close enough to Lawford Mountain to be practical. All the veterinarians do their best, but we need a place with specialists who were trained at rescue and rehabilitation. To reintroduce wild animals into their natural habitat. Whether it's a fox or a blue jay, there needs to be a place especially designed and geared for that purpose. Ideally there needs to be a preservation side for those animals that can't be reentered into their natural habitat."

Alan bobbed his head. "Makes a lot of sense. But it doesn't sound cheap."

"Not even a little bit." Cindy slid into the seat beside him and stabbed at the pasta in front of her. "It doesn't help any that this town, and this mountain, has already donated a nice chunk of change to the new cardiac wing at the local hospital."

"Yes, my grandfather mentioned something about that to me. Isn't the lead cardiac surgeon heading up the new team another one of the General's granddaughters?"

Cindy nodded. "My cousin Heather. What she's done is amazing."

"But you don't want to overtax people asking for donations."

She tapped the tip of her nose with her finger.

"This sounds like a fun idea." He waved the paper. "If I can help in any way."

"I'll let Nadine know she can count on you." The whole idea was a little more than funny. A few hours ago, she was ready to run for her life from the crazy man with tied up dummies and sharp knives, and now she was hoping to count on him to help make a dream come true. She stabbed at another bite of lasagna and wondered what else did this man have in store for her?

CHAPTER SEVEN

Much like yesterday, the words flowed freely from his fingertips to the keyboard and, praise heavens, the screen in front of him. Unlike yesterday, rather than run out of steam after the first hour, he'd been on such a roll this morning, he'd forgotten to stop and eat. Running on fumes from one large black cup of coffee, his body and his muse both cried out for food. And if he had this cat thing figured out correctly, he expected the kitten snoozing in his favorite box would shortly wake and join the *feed me* chorus.

Reluctantly, he pushed away from the table. There was only so much a man could accomplish on adrenaline and caffeine. Almost afraid that if he walked away from his keyboard, the ideas that had been bouncing about in his head like an old-fashioned pinball machine would literally fall out of his ears and not come back to play, he forced himself to slap together the fastest lunch possible.

It took him all of five seconds, maybe three, to calculate zapping the last piece of leftover lasagna would be faster than assembling the ingredients for a sandwich. The problem, of course, no matter which quick meal he chose, he might be able to type while he chewed, or perhaps type one handed, but neither would be able to capture the ideas as quickly as they came to mind. Years of experience told him that waiting until he could sit down uninterrupted would prove the most productive. Which left the question, how quickly could he shovel down a piece of lasagna?

Warmed plate in hand, he returned to the table and still standing, caught a glimpse of the view from the side window. The sunlight glittered on the lake. Had it been that sparkly yesterday? Leaves on neighboring trees waved in the light breeze of the day, and he was pretty sure even through the well-insulated glass, he could hear birds chirping delightfully. *Delightfully*? He had to laugh at himself. If he spent too much more time here in the middle of Mother Nature on steroids, he'd wind up a damn poet instead of a thriller writer.

Savoring the first bite of leftovers, he had to admit, Lucy's lasagna would take the prize over just about any Italian grandmother's cooking he'd ever had the pleasure of eating. His gaze returned out the window. How had he spent almost a month in this cabin, standing in this very spot, and never stopped to smell the proverbial roses?

Who knows, maybe his grandfather had been right in the first place. Maybe if he had spent less time pacing the wooden floors and staring at the pine paneling, and instead had sat on the porch or walked the trails, perhaps his muse would have returned weeks ago. On the other hand, he carried his plate out to the front porch, maybe his grandfather's second thought was more on point.

The timing of the return of his muse coincided with not only a breath of fresh air, but face-to-face interaction with the community. Well, at least two members of the community. The sweetest Irish lady he'd ever had the pleasure of meeting—even if she was a bit on the stubborn side, at least she didn't question his need for a twenty pound rib roast. And of course, the lovely veterinarian.

His mind lingering on Dr. Hyacinth Nelson, he sank into the forest green rocker. Stabbing at another morsel, he set the chair to rocking and decided perhaps a leisurely lunch with Mother Nature and Hyacinth Nelson, in spirit at least, wasn't a bad idea.

Savoring the last bite, and the view, the mewl of the hungry kitten called. It was time for him to get back to work anyhow. Pushing to his feet, he took one last look at the lake. It might be a good idea to make time to walk one of the paths that led around the shore. Maybe, he smiled, he could talk one pretty veterinarian into joining him. Yes, that was one walk that he would most certainly enjoy. Another mewl and he stopped short. His neck craned, he looked into the cabin at the tiny box, and the sleeping kitten.

"What the heck?"

Another sound and glancing over his shoulder, he searched for where the faint cry had come from. It took another minute and a few more mewls before another gray tabby appeared at the bottom step. *Uh oh.*

The same as he'd done yesterday, he slowly descended the steps and scooped the little guy up. "Something tells me we were searching for you last night." Scratching under the squirming kitten's chin, he glanced around for more siblings. Using his free arm, he shook the shrubs along either side of the porch steps. No sign of any movement.

Surely, if a mama cat had dropped this guy off, she would be somewhere nearby. Cell phone in hand, he dialed and slowly strolled the perimeter of the house for the best reception.

On the second ring, a familiar voice answered. "Lawford Veterinary."

"Hi. This is Alan." He cleared his throat. "I didn't expect you to answer the phone yourself."

"We are only open half a day on Saturday, and everybody else has gone home. I'm just finishing up some last-minute business, and then I was going to call you."

"Call me?" His heart did a little jig.

"Yes. Since you're so fond of my sister's baking, and she doesn't sell her *Apfel* kuchen at the bakery, the family thought you might enjoy joining us for supper tonight. The kuchen is for dessert."

"I'm sorry, the what?"

Cindy laughed. He really did like that laugh. The mere sound of it made him want to smile. "It's German apple cake. And seriously delicious. At least it is when she bakes it."

"I gather you don't bake?"

He could almost hear her head shaking. "Not for my worst enemy. My talents are not in the kitchen."

There was no way he was touching that statement with a ten foot pole. "Dinner sounds fine, but I may have a new complication."

"Oh, I'm sorry. You called me. What's up? Is it the kitten?"

"Not exactly."

A heavy sigh carried through the phone. "I'm really learning to not like when you say that. What exactly is wrong?"

"Wrong may be a misnomer. But you know that mama kitty we were looking for yesterday?"

"You found her!"

The words *not exactly* almost slipped past his lips. "No. But it seems our little guy has a sibling. And this guy is squirming a lot more. He's not very happy."

"Depending on how far he's traveled to find you and how long it's been since his mother left him or lost him, he or she is probably hungry. Go ahead and mix up some of the kitten mash like you've been feeding the other one. And I'll be there in about 20 minutes."

He bobbed his head. "Will do."

Slipping the phone back into his pocket, he continued his efforts to calm the little bundle of fur and made his way back up the porch. With this new arrival and Cindy on her way, he was unlikely to get any more writing done. The sound of her laughter replayed in the back of his mind. An image popped into his head of the cute way the bridge of her nose crinkled when something bothered her. Maybe this new turn of events wasn't such a bad thing at all.

● ● ● ●

"Are you sure they'll be fine?" Alan asked.

"Absolutely." Once she'd confirmed both kittens were doing well, she'd convinced Alan to let her show him the lake she'd grown up with firsthand.

"They're just so little." He shook his head.

Getting a kick out of this almost fatherly concern from the man who yesterday wanted absolutely nothing to do with one kitten never mind two, she parked behind Hart House and climbed out of the car. "Both are perfectly healthy. Well fed. And have each other to snuggle up to. We'll only be gone a short while, and then before supper tonight we'll double check on them, feed them again, and they'll probably be good for the night."

"I suppose if anybody would know, it would be you." He flashed a smile, no doubt intended to build confidence. Whether hers or his, she wasn't sure.

Just as they reached the front walk, Lucy came flying out the front door and nearly mowed the couple down. "Oh my, I'm so sorry."

"Slow down. What's wrong?" Lucy was rarely rattled, and seeing her in such a flurried state sent Cindy's internal alarms blasting.

"It's Adeline Taylor. That no good husband of hers."

"I thought she divorced him."

"She did. Things were going just fine too."

"But…?" She waited impatiently for the rest of the story.

"He took his bowling ball."

"What?" Alan looked more confused than she was.

"She got the contents of the house. He didn't remove his bowling ball. Afterwards when he asked for it and when she wouldn't give it to him, he waited for her to be out and let himself in to take it."

"She didn't change the locks?" It wasn't really a question. Adeline had always been a bit on the flighty side.

Hefting her purse over her shoulder again, Lucy shook her head.

"If I may ask," Alan looked from Cindy to Lucy, "why didn't she just give him the bowling ball?"

Lucy rolled her eyes. "Because that would have been too easy. Now she's having a minor melt down at the thought of being alone in the house until the locksmith comes. I shouldn't be very long."

"If it will help," Alan faced Lucy, "if she has a lock I'll be happy to change it for her."

A pleased smile spread across Lucy's face. "Isn't that nice of you. Thank you, but a phone call is already into the locksmith. I've got a nice bottle of wine in my bag. I'll have her calmed down and the locks changed in no time."

"If you're sure?" Alan waited.

"I'm sure. I feel better already knowing everything is taken care of." Lucy waggled her fingers at them and hurried up the hill to her car.

"All this commotion over a bowling ball." Alan tsked. "The husband isn't dangerous, is he?"

Cindy shook her head. "Not at all. If there were ever two people who were happiest fighting, it was them. If Adeline said the sky was blue, Ed said the sky was green, and they'd spend the next two days arguing over it. I'm not surprised even after the divorce they're still fighting."

"Now what?"

"To the boats." Cindy led the way down the point.

Looking from side to side, Alan nodded softly. "Boy, the view is just as beautiful from this vantage point as it is from on top of the hill."

"Absolutely. There's no such thing as a bad view on Lake

Lawford." Stopping on the edge of the stone wall, she waved an arm. "Your ride, sir."

Alan peered over the edge. "The canoe or the paddleboat?"

"Oh heavens, the paddleboat." She nudged him along the wall to the stairs. "If we took the canoe, knowing Lucy, she's liable to pop out from under the water and steal the oars."

"Why in heavens name would she do that?"

"It's a long story with its roots in an almost obsessive love of confined spaces and *Hello Dolly*."

Closing one eye, Alan studied her with the other one. "I'm not making the connection, and part of me isn't sure I want to."

"Now you're catching on." She laughed. "Let's just leave it at the truth really can be stranger than fiction."

"Don't I know that." He climbed into the small boat beside her and decided this was definitely a more pleasant way to spend the afternoon than staring at his computer screen.

Secured to the point by two ropes, the paddleboat rocked with her movement as she loosened the first tie. First rope undone, her phone rang and she juggled answering and untying the second. "Hello?"

"I'd swear if this head weren't attached to my shoulders it would roll off some days." Lucy sounded frantic. "I forgot the roast is in the oven on high temps to sear the juices. I need you to please lower it to 300 degrees. I'll adjust as necessary when I get back."

"Will do. Even I can manage that."

"Of course you can, dear. You're a doctor of veterinary medicine. The concept of turning a knob should not escape you. If I'm delayed for any reason, your grandmother and the General should be back from their monthly shopping spree to Boston in time to deal with dinner."

"Understood. Don't worry." The call disconnected, Cindy turned. "If you wait here one minute, I'm going to run back to the house and lower the oven temps. It shouldn't take me but a few minutes."

Moving quickly, Cindy hurried into the house, zeroed in on the large oven and quickly turned the knob down to 300 as requested. Spinning on her heel, she retraced her steps and smiled at the nice guy in the boat. Too bad he wasn't going to be around longer; she wouldn't mind getting to know him a lot better.

"That was quick." He reached out to help her into the boat.

"Now you'll get to see the lake up close and personal."

"Sounds good to me."

Together they pedaled away from the stone wall and made their way into the deeper water.

"It's amazing how small the main house looks from here, and yet it stands tall and proud nonetheless."

"Yes it does." From almost anywhere on the lake Hart House could be seen. Much of the shoreline had changed since her childhood, but not Hart Land. She took him on a path directly across and around into a familiar cove, then pointed. "See that?"

Alan squinted at the distance. "Am I looking for something in particular?"

"All of it." She waved her arm from left to right. "That used to be Carter land."

"Why does that sound familiar?"

"Did you read about the factory scandal? The spoiled rich brat who risked his family's legacy for some fast under the table money?"

"Oh, yes." He nodded. "My grandfather mentioned it. Something about illegal dumping."

"My cousin Violet's fiancé and his company have stepped in to expedite testing and clean up."

"Nice."

"More than nice. A huge portion of the land that was unaffected is going to be donated for the Lawford Mountain Preserve and Sanctuary. It's why that particular part of the dream has gone from a wish list to a countywide street fair."

Smiling at her, his gaze leveled more intensely on the landscape around them. "The flyer."

"It should be a blast. There are a handful of towns around the mountain that are going to be doing it on the same day. There's going to be petting zoos for the kids, and face painting, and there's a balloon artist coming, all of whom have donated their time, and all the stores will have their wares out in front and a percent of the profits are going to the construction fund for the first building."

"I don't know that I've ever been to a true small-town festival, but it sounds like it'll be very successful."

"I hope so. If we can raise enough to start with a small clinic and education center, I'll be thrilled."

"I'm willing to bet your sister's bakery alone is going to have a bumper crop of sales to donate. I'd like to help. It'll be a while before this next book is ready for sale, but I'd be honored if you'd let me earmark some of the earnings towards this project."

"That's very thoughtful of you." It made her heart light that so many people wanted to help with this dream of hers. Not that she expected much of a donation from a role-playing, aspiring author and a book that who knew if he'd ever get around to finishing. But still, it was the thought that counted. She was right from the beginning. Alan Peterson was just a really nice guy.

CHAPTER EIGHT

"I can certainly understand why you love the lake so much." Not since his brief stint as a Boy Scout had Alan played with knots. Well, that wasn't totally true. He had an occasion or two with Harvey, but not the same as tying a boat to a dock. Following Cindy up the ladder, he did his best to keep his eyes on his feet. The woman sure knew how to wear a pair of jeans. "I will admit, I should have gotten out of the cabin sooner."

"I hope this means you'll come back." At the top of the Point wall, she stood grinning down at him, her cheeks tinged a pale shade of pink.

If she kept looking at him like that he might not want to leave. "I hope so too."

"Good." She spun around and paused. Cocking her head to one side, she glanced at her watch. "It's been almost an hour. I would've thought somebody would be home by now."

"Maybe they are."

"No cars around."

"Does this mean you're making the sides for dinner?" he teased.

She turned to face him and continued walking backwards. "You really don't want that. Cooking edible meals and I are not on a first name basis."

"Not even a tossed salad?" He wondered how she wasn't tripping over the exposed roots and uneven ground below her. "Do you do this a lot?"

Her gaze narrowed at him. "Avoid cooking?"

"No." He pointed to the ground behind her. "Walk backwards without looking and without falling down."

"Oh, that." Again, she spun around, only this time took off running and called over her shoulder, "I can run with my eyes closed too."

By the time he caught up with her at the front porch, he was out of breath. It had been ages since he'd had to run anywhere. Even so, he couldn't stop laughing. When was the last time he'd had this much fun?

"Oh, no!"

The smell of burn and smoke slapped him in the face at about the same time Cindy made a dash across the foyer. The loud shrill enhanced the speed of his racing heart. Only a step behind her in the kitchen, he knew right away what the problem was. Tendrils of smoke seeped from the edges of the oven. "Don't open that!"

The hand holding a potholder froze midway to the offensive appliance. "Why?"

"It's contained. If you don't have a fire yet, letting oxygen in could start one. Give me a second." He quickly scanned the impressive kitchen and spotted the extinguisher. Grabbing it out of its holder, he moved quickly to her side. "I think I see the problem."

"The problem is the oven is on fire."

"Not quite." He turned to the two knobs and motioning for her to step aside, eased the door ajar. "Open the windows."

She tore off toward the sink and shoved open the first window, quickly gliding sideways toward the next. "What the hell happened?"

Hands covered with Teflon mitts, he waved the smoke away from his face a moment before pulling out the pan and setting it down on the stone beside him. A slab of charcoal stared back at him.

All the windows and back door now open, Cindy came to stand beside him. "It's ruined."

"Maybe." He turned on the fan and continued waving at the lingering smoke.

Her hands on her hips, Cindy shook her head. "There is no maybe about it. But why?"

"Wrong oven." He continued waving at the smoke, considering the options.

"I'm sorry. What?" Stepping back, Cindy picked up a card from the counter to help fan the smoke away.

"You turned the temperature knob on the lower oven." He pointed to the control on the upper left. "The roast was in the top oven." He shifted his finger to point to the right.

Cindy threw her head back and sighed. "This is why I don't

cook."

"Don't be so hard on yourself. Anyone could have made that mistake."

The glare she shot in his direction could have withered steel.

"Just trying to help."

"What are you doing now?" She continued to wave at the smoke. At least the danged alarm had stopped.

Stabbing at the charred meat with a large fork and knife, he pulled the roast apart. "Determining if we can salvage this."

"You're kidding?" Her eyes opened wide. "Or you're blind."

"No and no. And I think once we cut off the layers of black we can salvage enough for hash." Setting the utensils down beside him, he pushed his sleeves up and turned to her. "We've got work to do. I'll need some potatoes. Where's the pantry?"

She stood rooted to the floor. "You cook?"

"Don't look so surprised." He flashed his best impish grin. "I have to do something with all those practice roasts."

● ● ● ●

"Good grief, is Lucy sick?"

"Rose!" The familiar voice had Cindy spinning around and dropping the fan. Of all her cousins, Rose and Zinnia were the two that had the most difficulty making it back to the lake to visit. Having one of them here was more than a pleasant surprise. "What miracle happened to bring you here?"

"Oh Lord, don't ask." Twisting her long red hair into a bun and clipping it behind her head, Rose blew out a heavy sigh. "We've got two weeks until the new exhibit opens, we have a huge fundraising auction scheduled for this Thursday, and the blasted paintings are stuck in customs. Still."

"That doesn't sound good." Alan stood by the sink filling a pot with water for the potatoes.

Twisting around, Rose seemed to notice for the first time that somebody else was in the room. "Hi."

"I'm so sorry." Cindy extended her arm in Alan's direction. "This is Alan Peterson, a guest in the Aspen cabin." The same arm waived over to Rose. "And this is my cousin Rose. She's up from Boston."

"Nice to meet you," he said

"Same here," Rose agreed.

Cindy turned to her cousin. "So what does your artwork stuck in customs have to do with you finally coming to the lake?"

Even though she had no idea what was going on in the kitchen, just like every cousin who walked into the Hart domain before dinnertime, she shrugged into one of Lucy's oversized aprons and was ready to go to work. "There is no way it is clearing until Monday at the earliest, no matter how many frenzied or irate phone calls I make. And just in case you're wondering, threatening to send my retired Marine Corps general grandfather down to show them how to get things done doesn't help."

"No," Cindy tried not to laugh, "I wouldn't think that would have worked any better than had the U.S. Customs called the General and offered to show him how to get things done."

"Well, when you put it that way." Rose tied the apron behind her. "Anyhow, given the prospect of being chained to my desk able only to snarl at the phone, I figured the best medicine for my blood pressure would be to hightail it to the lake. After all, if I can do nothing to fix this mess from Boston, I might as well do nothing to fix this mess from Lawford."

"Good point."

"So," Rose rubbed her hands together briskly, "what can I do to help?"

Cindy held her hands up, palms out. "Don't look at me. I'm the reason we're not having Lucy's roast for dinner."

"Yeah," Rose chuckled, "I figured something like that might be what happened."

"Can you peel potatoes?" Alan asked.

"Can't everybody?" Rose teased, then turned to her cousin. "You should probably peel the potatoes. You can't cut off a finger with the potato peeler."

"Ha ha ha." At this point Cindy wasn't going to mention that her cousin was probably right. With the adrenaline rush of the last several minutes from trying not to burn the kitchen down, combined with the long busy morning at the clinic, she probably could easily slice off a finger instead of the potatoes.

Exchanging stories, the three of them worked, laughing, and teasing each other over captive art exhibits, life-like dummies, and burning dinner. By the time Rose finally stopped rolling with laughter over their guest caught stabbing at a twenty pound rib roast and scaring Cindy half to death, instead of charred kitchen, the house smelled like sautéed onions and roasted potatoes.

"What have we here?" Lucy stripped out of her sweater and set her bag on the counter.

Supervising from the kitchen table, Grams sat surrounded by piles of fabric squares. "The kids cooked dinner for us."

"Here you go, Grams." Poppy handed her grandmother the iron. "Don't look at me, I only got home about ten minutes ago."

Cindy shook her head. Not that there was a chance in hell that Lucy would think she'd had anything to do with actually cooking dinner. But if she was lucky, Lucy wouldn't realize that she was also the one responsible for almost ruining dinner. "I didn't even peel the potatoes. But I did set the table."

Sniffing at the air, Lucy followed her nose to the stove, almost dropping the pot lid when she spotted Rose coming from out of the pantry. "Oh my gosh, Rose. Honey, when did you learn how to cook?" The woman had actually said that with a straight face.

"As much as I would love to take credit for tonight's dinner creation, I can only lay claim to chopping potatoes and vegetables."

The frown descended on Lucy. "Then who…?"

Multiple fingers pointed at the only man standing in the room. Rinsing off a few dishes by the sink, Alan raised one hand and smiled at Lucy. "My grandmother always said *what good is a man if he's no good in the kitchen.*"

"Interesting philosophy," Lucy muttered, taking a wooden spoon and staring into the pot. "Do I want to know why my roast beef is now hash?"

Every head in the room shook from left to right, except for Alan who kept his gaze on his pot of hash. Cindy could almost feel everyone hold their breath as Lucy took a taste of Alan's efforts at salvaging supper.

"Oh, my." She took a second taste. "This is absolutely delicious."

"The secret is in the cream," Alan explained with a grin.

Lucy nodded. "You're going to have to give me the recipe."

"That can be arranged."

The clacking sound of paws against hardwood floors entered the kitchen seconds before the General turned the corner. "Are we planning on yakking about this dinner all night or are we going to sit down and eat it?"

Immediately, one by one, each member of the family's shoulders snapped erect. One *yes sir* followed another until everybody was seated at the large dining room table.

"Tell me, Alan," Grams dabbed the corners of her mouth with her napkin, "was it your grandmother or your mother who taught you how to cook like this?"

"Actually, neither. After college I learned rather quickly that unless I wanted to go broke eating out, I'd better learn how to cook."

"Well, I'm impressed. You can cook for us anytime you want." Grams turned to Cindy seated across from her. "And you, young lady, might want to take some lessons from this young man. Someday you are going to need to know how to cook *something*."

"And on that note," Poppy pushed to her feet and Cindy quietly mouthed thank you to her baby sister, "who wants dessert?"

Alan looked at his watch and then turned to Cindy. "It's been almost three hours. Maybe I should be getting back."

"We are having Lily's *apfel* kuchen," Poppy told him as if that were all he needed to know to change his mind.

"Warm." Lily carried a large pan into the dining room and set it down in the center of the table. "Dig in."

Cindy reached over and patted the top of his hand. "They'll be fine a little while longer."

"They?" Grams asked.

"Two kittens have adopted me," Alan explained, quickly adding, "temporarily."

That actually made Cindy laugh. She wasn't buying temporary anymore.

"Kittens," Grams said slowly. "We do seem to have an

abundance of them this spring, don't we?"

At the opposite end of the table, the General cleared his throat loudly. "I'll have a large piece, thank you."

"Any other takers?" Lily cut a piece of cake for her grandfather and handed the dish to him.

"A very good source says that I have time to enjoy one slice, please." Alan held up a plate for her.

Lily winked at Cindy and smiled. "Smart man. Not as smart as my Cole, but smart enough."

Handing her own dish over to her granddaughter, Grams looked to Alan. "What about the mama, did she adopt you too?"

"No. We haven't been able to find the mother cat."

The General coughed loudly.

"Are you still taking your allergy medicine?" Cindy asked. It had been quite some time since she'd heard the General coughing.

Slapping his hand against his chest, her grandfather shook his head. "No. Just went down the wrong pipe." He cleared his throat again. "You have time to join us for cards tonight?"

"No, I'm afraid I really should get home and check on the kittens." Alan swallowed his first taste of *apfel* kuchen. "And my compliments to the baker. You have outdone yourself."

Lily smiled. "It is a family favorite."

"Face it," the General beamed at his granddaughter, "pretty much everything you bake is a family favorite."

"Yes." Her grin widened. "It is."

Two more bites and Alan had practically inhaled his dessert. "I hate to eat and run, but I really should get back and check on the kiddos."

"Yes. I'll give you a ride." Cindy stood and turned to her grandparents. "It's been a very long day. I'm gonna head home after I drop him off."

"Will we see you tomorrow, dear?" Grams asked.

"Yes," Rose chimed in. "We have lots to catch up on."

When it came to the recent happenings in their lives, Cindy had a feeling she was going to be the *catchee* and Rose the *catchor*. She could see the curious gleam in her cousin's eyes. "Wouldn't miss it for the world."

Not man nor beast would keep her away from an afternoon with her cousins. Stepping away from the table, her eyes leveled with Alan's. Well, maybe one man.

• • • •

From where he stood on the veranda, the General had a perfect view of the front path, the side parking lot, and Cindy and Alan walking side by side.

His bride of decades came to stand behind him, resting her hand on his shoulder and leaning against him. "He is an interesting man, isn't he?"

"At least he can cook."

Fiona chuckled. "And quite well. Makes a woman wonder what other hidden talents the man might have."

One brow raised, he turned to look at his wife. Rolling her eyes, she chuckled, lightly smacking him on the shoulder. He chuckled back at her. Oh, how he loved this woman. It was beyond him how other men got through life.

He turned back in time to see their guest holding the car door for his granddaughter.

"Don't you think it's interesting that he's turned down a month of invitations, but accepts the first time Cindy extends the invite?" Fiona leaned in closer.

Yes, he thought it very interesting. Of course, he would have expected nothing less.

CHAPTER NINE

The last few days, Alan had actually looked forward to the morning. Not only had the kittens taken to curling up on the pillow beside him, one of the two gray fur balls occasionally liked strolling over to his pillow and sprawling out above his head. He didn't mind the kitten seeking out his warmth, it was the rumbling purr in the middle of the night that still startled him out of a sound sleep. Despite the interrupted rest, his morning routine now included at least a couple of hours of putting words on a page. At this pace, he'd have the book finished in no time.

For some reason, that thought didn't make him nearly as happy as it should. And why was that a surprise to him? Finishing the book meant no more reason to stay. No reason to stay meant no more time with Hyacinth Nelson. That idea was enough to make him want to slam his laptop shut and take a stroll in the woods. Or maybe a ride into the other side of town. He could take the two kittens for a checkup of sorts. Now that was an idea that really put a smile on his face.

"What do you think about that?" Using his pointer finger, he scratched behind the ear of the darker gray kitty. Curled in his favorite box, the only reaction the kitten offered was to stretch his neck further out for more scratches. Not even the knock at the door captured the animal's interest.

Now that he had met so many more people in the community and come out of his cave, so to speak, he had no idea who could be knocking. Though he had his hopes.

The front door open, he was delighted to find one smiling veterinarian standing like an angel with the sunlight shining behind her. Boy, if he stayed much longer, he really was going to become a poet.

"I'm not interrupting, am I?"

He waved her inside. "Not at all."

"I have a few people I need to see in town to follow up on the sidewalk fair, and thought I'd pop in first to see how Frick and Frack are doing."

"Frick and Frack." He chuckled and shook his head. "Not sure how I feel about the names, but they say great minds think alike. I was just considering bringing the kittens in for a checkup."

"Glad I could save you a trip." She followed him inside. "I see this is still their favorite spot."

"I was surprised one could fit in that box. I can't believe two of them are in there."

"You'd be amazed. We once spent almost an hour trying to find a missing kitten. My receptionist was in a total state of frenzy. She blamed herself for not keeping a closer eye on the kittens."

"But you did find him?"

She nodded. "Yeah, he crawled into a tissue box and had fallen asleep."

"I can see how he might've been overlooked." He chuckled. No wonder so many people found kittens irresistible. He was quickly becoming one of them. Already he was starting to wonder who would become these little animals' people. A part of him wanted to have approval rights. And wasn't that ridiculous. This wasn't a film contract that gave him casting rights. "Would you like a cup of tea, glass of water, coffee?"

Cindy lifted one of the kittens, rubbed its tummy, and shook her head. "How is the litter box working out?"

What kind of a question was that? "Fine?"

"Are you asking me or telling me?" She smiled up at him. He really was getting much too used to that smile.

"I suppose I'm telling you. At least, I haven't found any droppings around the cabin. And there seems to be a reasonable amount of clumping. At least I think it's reasonable."

"Good." She held up the darker gray kitten, nibbling on her finger. "This little guy is a feisty one, isn't he?"

Alan chuckled. "Yeah. I noticed that too. I'm not positive but I'm pretty sure he's the one who likes to attack my toes while I'm sleeping, and the other fellow is the one who likes to purr on my head."

"I could see that." She laughed with him.

He stole a quick glance at the clock over the table, thinking quickly how to extend his time with her. "Since it's almost lunchtime, I was thinking of checking out Mabel's. Any chance I can steal you away for a short while?"

Flipping her wrist, Cindy glanced at her watch and nodded. "I think I can make that work."

"Great, your car or mine?"

"We'll take mine," she said. "I know how to get from here to town with my eyes closed."

Placing his hand at the small of her back, he ushered her out the door, shaking his head. "If you don't mind, I'd rather you kept your eyes open."

They laughed the short distance to the car, threw out awful cat name suggestions during the drive, and were still laughing as they walked up the stairs into the diner.

Eyes shimmering with curiosity, a waitress quickly crossed the restaurant in their direction. "Isn't it nice to see you in here."

According to the woman's name tag, she was the reason for the pink neon Mabel's sign. Her gaze immediately shifted to Alan, and exactly the way he might have described in one of his books, each corner of her mouth slowly tilted up into a grin that shouted he and the doc would be on the next grapevine broadcast.

Mabel and Cindy exchanged friendly banter on the way to a booth near the back corner. After Mabel handed each of them a menu, she looked back at him, the sparkle in her eye disappearing. "What would you like to drink?"

"Water for me," Cindy said.

"Me too."

"Two waters coming up." Mabel nodded. "I'll be back to take your orders in just a minute."

"So," fingers laced in front of her, Cindy leaned forward, "you don't like Batman and Robin?"

"Nope. One of them would be bound to have an inferiority complex."

Shaking her head, Cindy muffled a laugh, much the way she'd done the entire car ride here. "Then I guess Holmes and Watson are out of the question?"

"But Sherlock and Holmes would work."

"I like Snoopy and Charlie Brown better."

This time he shook his head. "Charlie Brown is too long. He'd wind up just being Charlie. And Snoopy is a dog."

"Garfield?" she asked.

Mabel appeared, setting a glass of water in front of each of them, her gaze remaining steady on Alan. Whatever she was sizing up, he had a feeling the afternoon's grapevine was going to be seriously buzzing. "Do you know what you'd like to eat?" she asked.

"I'll have grilled cheese with bacon, a side of sweet potato fries, and a slice of blueberry sour cream pie."

"That's what I love about you Nelson girls. None of that salad and diet stuff." Mabel turned to Alan.

"That sounds delicious. I'll have the same."

Mabel nodded, stared at him one long second, and then scurried away.

"Does she look at everybody that way?"

Cindy shrugged. "Maybe she agrees with me and thinks Snoopy and Charlie Brown are good names."

A loud shriek boomed from the kitchen. All heads turned to the kitchen doors that flew open, banging against the cabinets at either side, and Mabel spewing forth full speed ahead. *Now what*?

● ● ● ●

"Oh. My. God. It *is* you!" Clutching something to her chest, Mabel came to a screeching halt at their table and shoved whatever she'd been holding along with a pen under his nose.

Cindy didn't know whether to duck under the table or give the woman a tranquilizer.

Patting her chest with one hand and waving under her chin with the other, the diner owner looked ready to hyperventilate. "I can't believe it. Oh my. I love your books. My sister is never going to believe this. Alan Peters in my diner."

Peters? *Wasn't he Peterson*?

"Would you please sign this?" Mabel actually blushed. "That's

Mabel, M.A.B.E.L."

"Of course." He smiled up at her, cast a quick glance and apologetic shrug at Cindy, then bowed his head and scribbled something inside the hardcover book.

Alan Peters? *Holy…*

The kitchen bell echoed through the open doorway and Mabel's brows shot up high on her forehead. "That's your lunch. I will be right back." She did a military turn on her heel and scooted across the dining area, ignoring all questions from concerned customers.

"I hate to say this," Alan sighed, "but there's a really good chance we're not going to have a very peaceful lunch."

"Good Lord. You're a writer." Nothing like stating the obvious.

Confusion stared back at her. "I told you I was a writer."

"Yeah, but you didn't tell me you were a real writer."

Leaning back in the booth, Alan bit back a smile. "As opposed to a fake writer?"

Cindy, on the other hand, leaned forward and lowered her voice. "As opposed to a really bad writer who doesn't sell books. You're famous."

"Fame is in the eye of the beholder." He shrugged.

"I never have time to read and even I know who Alan Peters is."

A huge grin took over his face. "You do?"

She resisted the urge to roll her eyes at him. "Your books have been on the *New York Times* bestseller list steadily for years. Your name rolls off the tongue alongside the likes of James Patterson, Lee Child, or Dan Brown. Of course I know who Alan Peters is." Well— his books anyway. And then it hit her. He'd offered to donate proceeds from his next book to *her* project. Now she was the one who might hyperventilate.

"Are you okay?" Alan leaned in. "All the color just slid away from your face. I've written that, but I've never actually seen it."

Raising her hands to her cheeks, she nodded her head and snapped her mouth shut. "I was just thinking about your donation."

Relief washed over his face. "You scared me for a minute."

"Here we go." Mabel set the dish down in front of each of them, but grinned at Alan. "I had Jimmy on the grill give you extra fries." She winked. "No additional charge."

Keeping an eye on Mabel as she shuffled across the diner, Alan waited until she was completely out of earshot to lean forward again and speak. "Since I'm pretty sure that by the time I finish this sandwich the entire town is going to know that I'm here, what do you think of adding a book signing booth to the street fair?"

"You'd do that?" The thought *really nice guy* flashed to the forefront of her mind.

His head tipped slightly to one side and his brows crinkled. "Why wouldn't I want to?"

Cindy folded her fingers together and sucked in a deep breath. "This may be the most activity our little town bookstore has ever seen." She picked up her grilled sandwich, almost too excited to eat. "As soon as we're done here we'll hit Buy the Book."

Grilled cheese halfway to his mouth, his hands froze. "I gather that's the name of the bookstore?"

"It is."

"B Y or B U Y?"

"B U Y. Though I believe *buy buy* was in contention instead of *buy the*. At least that's the way the story goes, but it's been Buy the Book for as long as I can remember."

"However it's spelled, I'm glad to do something for a good cause and to support a local bookstore. As far as I can tell, it's a win-win for everyone."

"Here, here." She raised her glass of water and took a bite of her grilled cheese. Mouth full, she heard the sound of someone clearing their throat too close for comfort. Glancing up to her left, a young woman she didn't recognize stood beside them.

"I'm sorry to interrupt your lunch, but could I have your autograph please?" The young lady sported a shaky smile.

"Of course." By the time he handed back the signed napkin, a short line had formed behind him. The poor guy wasn't going to get much chance to eat at all.

Taking another bite of her sandwich, Cindy glanced at the growing line and realized they had a whole new publicity angle to add to their promotions. If she'd had any concerns before about turning a reasonable profit, they just flew out the window. Thank heaven for nice guys.

CHAPTER TEN

"**D**id you know?" Hands on her hips, Cindy stood in front of her grandparents.

Carefully pinning two fabric squares together, Grams glanced up at her. "Know what, dear?"

"That your guest in the Aspen cabin is a world famous mystery writer."

"Is he?" The General looked a tad too surprised.

"Isn't that nice." Her grandmother resumed sliding pins into the squares.

Lucy came through the doorway carrying a tray of her fresh squeezed lemonade. "Isn't what nice?"

The screen door swung open, and her red hair blowing in the breeze, Rose came flying inside. "Is it true?"

Cindy didn't have to ask what her cousin was talking about. "Yes."

"Is what true?" Lucy set the tray down on the table and straightened, fisting both hands onto her hips. "And isn't what nice?"

Rose whirled around to face Lucy. "The crazy roast stabbing and dummy loving guest in the Aspen cabin is the world famous mystery writer, Alan Peters."

In all her years, Cindy didn't think she had ever seen Lucy's eyes circled so big and round. The woman's jaw actually dropped open. Any minute now she'd be catching flies.

"Speaking of which," the General set his tablet aside, "where is our renowned guest?"

"He didn't want to leave the kittens too long again, so they're installed upstairs in the last bedroom. I left him washing his hands."

The screen door swung open again. This time Ralph came through the door with Thelma and Louise on his tail. "Ned and Nadine are parking their car."

Of course, after news spread through town like wildfire, this afternoon's card game would turn into a full house.

Looking around the room, Thelma practically shoved Louise out of the way. "Where is he?"

"He will be here any minute." Cindy put on her stern veterinarian face. "Can we please not all act like a pack of rabid hyenas?"

"I beg your pardon?" Her grandmother's hands stilled as she leveled her gaze on her granddaughter.

"I just want everybody to act perfectly normal around him. No bombarding him with requests for autographs—" The sounds of Thelma and Ralph snapping their fingers as if they'd missed out on the winning lottery numbers cut into her words. "No taking pictures, no peppering him with questions, *and* no more requests to read your unfinished manuscript."

"Who did that?" Poppy came out to the porch from inside.

Lifting her hands high into the air, Cindy let them drop in a fast—and frustrated—whoosh. "Apparently, we have more wanna-be writers in this town than I ever could have dreamed. He dropped off a stack of at least eight manuscripts when we picked up the kittens."

"Really?" Rose looked to her cousin.

"Why would I lie?"

"Is someone's pants on fire?" Alan stepped onto the porch. "The kittens seem very happy. One went left, the other went right, they sniffed along the perimeter, met in the middle and promptly fell over sound asleep."

Her grandmother's hands stilled on her lap, and Grams smiled up at no one in particular. "Don't you just love it when they do that?"

"They are rather cute," Alan admitted.

The General handed Alan a cold drink and set a deck of cards at each table. "Do the kittens have names yet?"

"I thought it best to wait for whoever is going to become their forever home to name them."

"Brilliant idea. Speaking of which, I have another one." Rose took a seat at one of the tables. "This Thursday night the museum is having a gala dinner auction. We're expecting some of the museum's biggest donors. One in particular I happen to know is a huge fan of Alan Peters."

"Oh," Grams glanced up from the pincushion, "I like where you're going with this."

Rose smiled at her grandmother and turned to Cindy. "I know I mentioned before that you should come and mingle with our guests, and just happen to mention the wildlife project." She turned momentarily to her partner in cards across the table. "After all, animals are a favorite cause of the philanthropic set. Anyhow, I think if you come and bring Alan, we can really get some buzz going for your fundraiser."

"I don't know." Cindy sucked in a deep breath. "First of all, these people, regardless of how much money they have, don't have bottomless pockets. Either they're going to give to your fundraiser for the museum or mine. And frankly, I feel like showing up to pinch your guests' wallets is a bit like poaching."

Swallowing a chuckle, Alan smiled at her. "No offense intended, but have you ever considered being a writer?"

Cindy rolled her eyes, choosing to accept the comment as a compliment rather than a tease. "Can't say that I have."

"Personally, I think it's a good idea." Alan shrugged at her. "I mean, the part about going to the gala."

"Isn't it enough that you are now reading a bunch of strange peoples' half written books. Probably, may I point out, badly written books."

He shrugged again. "You never know. One of them might be good."

The man seriously was way too nice. How had she ever thought he could possibly be a serial killer? "Okay, maybe. But even so, on top of reading these manuscripts, finishing your own book, you're also doing a book signing for the street fair. Don't you think that's enough?"

"Sweetie." Grams hands came to rest on her lap. "While I do understand your concern about taking advantage of Mr. Peterson's generosity with his time, perhaps you should look at the gala not so much as a work effort but a fun evening at a lovely party. After all, Rose does throw lovely parties."

"See!" Rose flashed her cousin a huge toothy grin.

Heads around the room nodded their agreement. It looked like she'd been outnumbered.

• • • •

"I think he's been holding out on us." Thelma tossed the last of her cards onto the table.

Ralph scribbled the new score onto the scratchpad. "He did say he knew how to play."

"Yeah," Louise reached for the new deck, "but he didn't say he knew how to play *that* well."

"Didn't you mention you were a military brat?" Ned asked from the next table.

Alan nodded. Considering Ned was the one with the worst hearing on the porch, he was the only one who seemed to have paid any attention when Alan had explained where he'd learned to play whist. "I am, but my grandfather is the one responsible for teaching me. He loved to play."

"That's right." Ned nodded. "An Annapolis grad. Everyone I ever met who graduated from the Naval Academy seems to have mastered the game."

"Are we going to yak all night, or are we going to play?" The General shoved the deck of cards in Ned's direction. "Cut," he ordered sternly.

"Heather just called," Lucy announced from the doorway. "A patient took a bad turn last night, and she needs to stay nearby."

"It sure will be nice when the new wing of the hospital is done." Poppy flopped into one of the rockers. "I know that Heather was worried things wouldn't happen quickly, but it was absolutely amazing how much money the fundraiser brought in. I still can't believe groundbreaking is in a few weeks."

"And with the warm weather season upon us," Louise dealt the cards, "there's a good chance the job will be done by winter."

Thelma picked up a card. "Maybe Rose should consider going into the fundraising business instead of the museum business."

Rose shook her head. "No, thank you. First off, I wouldn't know a darn thing about it if not for the museum and all the functions they throw to keep their patrons happy and bring in the funds for the bigger exhibits. Secondly, I only put what I've learned to use with people I love and thankfully I'm running out of people I love who need to raise money."

"I don't know about that." Grams blew out a slow sigh. "I'm a tad concerned about Zinnia. I think she's floundering a little."

"What exactly is she doing now?" Thelma asked.

"None of us are terribly sure." The General dealt out the last cards. "She's been rather secretive. Excited, but secretive."

"And you know," Grams said, "if the General can't maneuver details out of her, none of us will."

Lucy laughed. "Ain't that the truth."

The storm door slammed shut. Still dressed in shorts and a T-shirt, her blonde hair in her usual ponytail, Callie threw her arms up in the air. "We won!"

"And you're back earlier than we expected." Grams tipped her head in anticipation of a kiss on her cheek.

"Amazingly enough, every kid was accounted for and on their way home within minutes of stepping off the bus. I decided whatever needed to be organized post-win could wait till tomorrow. I'm hungry and tired." Callie dropped into the rocker beside her grandmother and sister.

"Anyone hear from Lily?" Lucy asked.

"Oh, sorry." Poppy raised a hand. "She didn't want to make anyone else stay after closing so she's waiting for someone from the PTA to pick up their order for tonight's concert."

"What concert?" Cindy asked.

Multiple heads turned to look at her. Some wide-eyed, some shaking, others merely rolling their eyes.

"Tonight is the first summer music night." Nadine reminded her. "I'm just glad I'm not on duty tonight."

"Music night?" Alan asked.

Poppy smiled up at him. "Yes, the first Sunday of every month during the warm weather season, the town brings in some band to play at the gazebo. They set up a dance floor and everything."

"Some bands work out better than others." Thelma rearranged her cards. "I bid four."

"The band they had at the end of last summer was fantastic."

Callie stretched her arms and set the rocker in motion. "Not too fast, not to slow, a nice blend of music for all ages."

"Yes, that's what the music committee is rooting for," Nadine reassured.

"Hmm," Poppy said. "Maybe we should check it out."

"That's what I was just thinking." Callie bobbed her head and turned to Cindy. "What about you?"

Instinctively her gaze shifted to Alan and quickly back to her cousin. What did it mean that what she really wanted to say was only if he does? "Could be fun."

"What about you, Mr. Superstar?" Rose asked.

"Superstar?" Callie followed Rose's gaze. "Did I miss something?"

Snickers of muffled laughter filled the air and a dash of pink eased up Alan's neck. "The cat—so to speak—has been let out of the bag that my pen name is Alan Peters."

Callie's eyes rounded big and wide. "Man, one day at a track meet and the biggest thing to hit this town since Grant showed up in a Lamborghini happens."

His gaze shifted momentarily to Cindy, at least she thought it did, before he faced Rose. "I think it sounds like fun."

Had the man who'd hibernated in his cabin for almost a month really just said that an open air concert with half the town would be fun?

"Great!" Poppy spun about. "I'd better go help Lucy get dinner on the table!"

Cindy followed after her sister. Suddenly, going to a crowded summer dance sounded like the most fun she would ever have in her life.

• • • •

Compared to sharing dinner with the family the night before, the gathering of both friends and family for a meal tonight was louder, busier, more chaotic, but just as fun. Alan couldn't remember the last time he'd felt more at home at a dining table, or laughed more over a meal. Well, not before today. This afternoon, lunch and cat names and one very lovely blonde animal doctor now strolling beside him down Main Street, had definitely been one of the best meals he could remember. Even with the unexpected revelation of his pen name.

"Oh, look." Poppy pointed up the street at the fire department vehicles parked ahead. "I wonder if Cole is on duty tonight?"

"Cole?" Alan leaned in and whispered to Cindy. He didn't remember any mention of other members of the family.

"Lily's fiancé," she answered back.

Now he remembered. Somewhere in all the conversations during the last two days, the subject of who was engaged to whom had come up and he had taken note of a fireman. In the back of his mind, he'd filed the information as a good reason to do a firehouse thriller. If nothing else the research would give him a valid excuse to come back to Lawford. Soon.

"How are the renovations coming on Violet's studio?" Poppy slowed her pace to match Rose's.

"Fortunately, she and Grant aren't the ones doing the actual work."

"Excuse me?" Callie raised a brow at her cousin.

Rose rolled her eyes. "I think it's great that my sister is over the moon in love with a guy who can't live without her, but so far I have yet to see them stand more than an inch apart from each other, and I'm pretty sure they haven't eaten a meal alone in weeks. When I called to see if she wanted to hitch a ride up here this weekend, she had to take a rain check because they were going to some cousin of Grant's birthday party on the Cape."

"At least she gets along well with his side of the family," Cindy offered.

"I suppose." Rose's agreement sounded less than convincing.

"Besides," Poppy picked up the pace, "aren't you always too busy with work?"

One side of Rose's mouth tipped up in a bashful smile as she repeated, "I suppose."

"Mm," Poppy countered, her grin beaming with satisfaction. Sounds of matching notes trickled in the air and Poppy looped her arm with her sister. "They're starting. We'd better hurry."

The two sisters took off galloping up the street, Callie pausing long enough to grab onto Rose and drag her behind them, leaving Alan and Cindy walking unaccompanied.

"Hey." Lily's voiced sounded over his shoulder seconds before she and a man he assumed had to be Cole came running up beside them holding hands. "Better pick up the pace. Don't want to miss the beginning or you won't be able to get near the dance floor." Not waiting for a response, giggling like a couple of little kids, the two continued up the street at a fast clip.

"What do you say?" He held his hand out to Cindy and mentally crossed his fingers.

Her hand slid into his. "Glad I wore comfortable shoes!"

So was he. They'd trotted past Lily and the fireman and the rest of the clan to arrive laughing and out of breath. "I am seriously going to need to work on my endurance if we're going to keep this up."

The first tune played in earnest. A classic from his mother's era, the song was just fast enough to want to tap your toes and just slow enough not to be off-putting. That was a good thing. The bad thing was that he wished he'd paid more attention to the cotillion dance lessons his parents had thrust upon him in his teens.

Except for Cole, who hadn't broken a sweat on the jaunt up the street, the others arrived to join them, laughing and breathing hard. Apparently he wasn't the only one with a sedentary job.

"What we need," Rose looked around, "is some refreshments."

"Good idea," Callie agreed, zeroing in on a booth across the way. "There." Like a parade, each of the Hart grandchildren and guests fell into step behind the high school coach.

A popular top forty song came on and Alan could see Cindy's toe tapping as she swallowed a long gulp of water. Within moments they'd lost Callie and Rose to the dance floor.

"This band is pretty good. I hope they'll all be like this." Poppy bobbed her head to the rhythmic beat.

"I wonder if they do weddings?" Lily asked. So far, with a little help from her sisters, she'd managed to organize and plan what was looking to be the perfect summer wedding, but what to do about music was still in the undecided column and they were running out of time.

A big beefy hand appeared in front of the younger sister. "May I have this dance?"

Poppy's gaze followed the edge of his fingertips up to his neck stopping at a wide smile. "Peyton! I would love to." The two disappeared into the crowd on the temporary wooden dance floor.

"Are you going to let your buddy show you up?" Lily turned to her fireman.

Extending his elbow to her, he flashed a smile that outshone his buddy. "Not on your life."

The sound of a finger tapped on the public announcement system. "Ladies and gentlemen, we are going to be starting this evening out with a little dance off. Grab a number and your partner and join us on the floor."

The way Cindy's face lit up, he knew she was antsy to join her sisters and cousin on the dance floor. Two left feet be damned, he wasn't about to disappoint her. "Shall we?"

That smile he loved so much appeared, making any impending embarrassment worth it. "Absolutely."

They had managed a sloppy rendition of the twist, and absolutely hilarious attempts at the chicken dance. He just prayed nobody had a camera pointed at him. That was followed by the monster mash. Until a few minutes ago, he didn't even realize there was a dance that went with the song. But the pièce de résistance had to be whatever line dance played that required moving forward, backward, sidestep, sidestep, spinning left, spinning right and had enough people laughing and tripping over each other that the judges had been tapping away, decreasing the number of contestants.

Alan had never been happier to hear a slow-moving tune that warranted putting his hands on Cindy without getting his face slapped, and a chance to catch his breath. What he hadn't bargained for was how good it would feel to have the small of her back under his fingertips.

"I didn't think they were ever going to slow down." Cindy took in a slow deep breath and let it out just as slowly.

"I know what you mean."

A couple on his right bumped into them, and Alan shifted left. Another couple looked to be almost asleep on their feet, when Alan pulled Cindy in more tightly barely avoiding a collision when the tired duo swayed into their dance space.

Startled blue eyes stared up at him.

"Sorry," he mumbled, about to loosen his hold when the same couple shifted and bounced into Cindy.

This time his dance partner's mouth popped open wide as her hand clutched at his shoulder.

Prepared to spin her away, he made one critical mistake. The same mistake every hero made in every cheap romance novel he'd ever read. He looked into those still startled blue eyes and let his gaze fall to luscious pink lips. Sucking in a deep breath, he'd just about won the battle of good angel bad angel, prepared to do the chivalrous thing and step back when perfectly straight white teeth nibbled on that pretty pink lower lip.

He was officially in over his head. Leaning forward, he kept his gaze locked on hers, searching for any sign that he was about to get his face slapped. Her mouth snapped shut and startled eyes grew dark and intense. She wasn't going to stop him and he had never been so damn glad about anything in his life.

The sweet soft kiss lasted longer than it should have, but not nearly as long as he would have liked. A loud throat cleared from either side of him and he realized that he'd been flanked by Cole and his buddy. Both staring daggers at him.

"Should I apologize," he spoke softly.

Cindy shook her head. "Only if you don't do it again." She turned her head left then right. "Perhaps somewhere more private next time."

The corners of his mouth pulled high against his cheeks and he was pretty sure there was a serious possibility his face might split wide open. There were several truths in this world. Life, death, taxes, bestseller lists, and for better or worse, he was seriously falling for one Hyacinth Nelson.

CHAPTER ELEVEN

The evening country dance and the chance to laugh with and have a legitimate excuse to hold Cindy had ended way too early for Alan. When they'd arrived at Hart house to pick up the kittens, the porch was still clamoring with people playing cards. Much to his chagrin, talking in private with Cindy would not happen. Any hope of getting a few minutes alone with her after he'd collected the kittens had been shot to hell when it was determined both Thelma and Louise had had a little bit too much to drink. Of course he'd known that the second he'd walked past the Merry Widow's table and Thelma pinched his rear. Louise's immediate shout of "You go, girl!" had cemented his, and everyone else's conclusions. Somehow Cindy wound up designated chauffeur.

With the kittens hungry and mewling loudly in the car, he along with Frick and Frack were the first to be dropped off. For the first time, the cabin looked unusually small. Adrenaline still high from having Cindy in his arms, even if it was on a public dancefloor, and the taste of her lips lingering on his mouth, there had been little point in going to bed. Instead, he spent hours in his chair, fingers on the keyboard, pretending to write. Tired of typing and deleting only to find himself still staring at blank pages, and after both kittens had curled up for the night, Alan finally gave up any pretense of work and crawled into bed. The next few hours were spent tossing and turning in pursuit of sleep.

By the time the sun rose, he wasn't sure that he'd gotten more than a few minutes of restless sleep. What he was sure of was that he'd spent most of the night, both awake and in sleep, with images of Cindy Nelson playing on a never ending loop. How had she managed to get so deep under his skin in such a short amount of time?

Hovering over the coffee maker, dark roast wasn't the only thing percolating this morning. New ideas were dancing around in his head faster than he could collect and record them. Pouring the coffee, scooping the sugar, retrieving milk from the refrigerator, scene after scene played out before him. The only problem being, the scenes had nothing to do with his current work in progress. The best he could come up with was that after hours of trying to make his fingers cooperate with the keyboard, and dreaming of Cindy, his subconscious must have put the two together and come up with a humdinger of a premise for a cozy mystery. He could picture it all so very clearly. The amateur sleuth, a country veterinarian, and her array of forest animals would stumble upon dead bodies all over her country mountain. And of course, her menagerie of forest friends would help solve the crimes. The whole concept seemed to be a warped rendition of a children's fairytale and an animated movie with a twist of classic TV and its talking horse.

Since the only thing he'd drank last night was lemonade, he couldn't even blame the odd river of current ideas on a hangover. But the even crazier thing was how sure he felt that he could make this lighter, more humorous storytelling work. Coffee mug in hand and the jolt of caffeine from his first few swallows in place, he needed to record the details of all the scenes racing around while they were still fresh in his mind. And of course, file them for another day. The same mind that was smart enough to recognize the only change in his life, the only difference between mental block and a river of ideas, had been the addition of Cindy in his world.

Refilling his mug and making his way over to the table, Alan took a seat and placed his hands on the keyboard. Not till Frick, or was it Frack, had curled up against his arm did he realize he'd only seen one kitten this morning. That was odd. The two were inseparable. And now that he thought about it, neither of the kittens had taken the time to curl up near his head last night. At the time he'd thought it due to his restless movements, but now he wasn't so sure. Could the other kitten have gotten out? He looked quickly at the closed front door and then scanned the windows, searching for any crack or crevice large enough for a small cat to climb up to and sneak out of.

"Where are you?" he mumbled mostly to himself, yet still hoping the kitten would come out when called. The other fellow popped up and stretching his chin, focused on him and let out an elongated meow. If Alan didn't know better, he'd swear the kitten was complaining what had taken him so long to look for his brother.

As if aware someone was looking for him, the missing kitty appeared in the hall. His steps slow and strained and after only taking a few, he collapsed on the floor. Not the cute way when they fell over sleeping, but like a dying man in the desert only a few feet from the life saving oasis. Alan's heart took off at rapid clip to match the speed with which he raced down the tiny hallway. Scooping the kitten up, panic nipped at his already fast ticking heart. The poor thing's eyes were glazed and droopy and Alan didn't need to be a veterinarian to know something was definitely very wrong.

Glancing up at the clock, he wondered just how early did country vets start their day? Not that he had much of a choice, working or not, he had to call Cindy. Now.

Cell phone in hand, every ring seemed to take an eternity. How he hated the idea of waking her up, but the kitten needed her.

"Hello." Her voice came across bright and chipper and not showing any signs of losing sleep the way he had. Too bad.

"Hi. Listen we have a new kitten problem."

"You found another one!" Her voice rose several octaves.

"No." His gaze shot to the front porch. At least he didn't think any more had appeared. "One of these guys is sick. I'm afraid very sick."

"What happened?" Seriousness crept instantly into her tone.

Snuggling the little guy against his chest, he scratched behind the kitten's ear with his thumb. "He can barely walk. On his way to me or the water bowl, not sure which, he just collapsed. He seems to be smacking his lips as though he's hungry or—"

"Thirsty," she cut him off.

"Yeah, Can you come and see?"

"I can, but I think it might be better if I meet you at the clinic. Do you think you can find it?"

"Yes." Thankfully on her trek to finalize details for the sidewalk festival, she'd taken the time to point out the clinic up the hill from Main Street. He remembered the location because the famed Floyd's barbershop anchored the corner spot.

"Any other symptoms? Sneezing, runny nose. Anything like

that?"

"His eyes are closed, but I think they're sort of oozing."

"Good. Very good. If it's his kidneys, we're in trouble. See you shortly!"

As much as he now realized he needed Cindy, this little guy needed her more. Suddenly the thought of losing either one of them stabbed sharply at his chest. Apparently he'd fallen head over heels for all three of them.

• • • •

As fast as she could, Cindy threw on a pair of jeans and made a beeline out the door. From the description of symptoms Alan had given her, the first thing that came to mind was a bad kidney. At this age, that would mean certain death for Frick or Frack. She hated losing an animal—any animal—but these guys had found a special place in her heart. Even in her dreams. This morning she'd woken with images of herself, Alan, and two playful kitties romping down Main Street. Of course the idea of romping in town with two cats was ridiculous, but wasn't that what dreams were for, impractical perfection.

Already waiting for her at the front door, Alan stood cradling a blanket smothered kitten. The totally distraught look in his eyes gave her heart a squeeze. She was going to have to find something else to call him besides a seriously nice guy. But he *was* seriously nice and she seriously wished he wasn't going to be leaving soon.

Keys in hand, she paused a moment and pulled back the blanket to better see the kitten's face. She was greeted by a sneeze. Another good sign. "Bless you."

"He's been doing that the entire car ride."

Cindy bobbed her head. "That's actually a good thing. It sounds like he's probably got some kind of an upper respiratory infection. Let's get this guy inside for a closer look.

"Thank you."

"That's what I'm here for." The smile that spread across his face did little to ease the concern in his eyes, but it did more to lift her mood than all the sunrises on the lake.

"So if all he has is a bad cold, we're doing good?" Alan asked.

Without slowing her pace, she dropped her purse and keys on the counter and proceeded to the closest exam room. Waving Alan inside, she explained. "If he can't smell, he won't eat or drink which makes dehydration a concern."

"But he was fine yesterday so he couldn't have gone without that much water, right?"

"His size is an issue. Let's see what we have." The first thing she did was to pinch the skin on the back of his neck and tried not to sigh. Rather than fall flat the way it should have, it remained taught in place. However long he'd gone without water, had been too long.

"What was that for?"

"Standard test for dehydration."

"And?"

"I'm going to have to give him an IV to re-hydrate."

Alan winced. "I should've paid more attention."

She shook her head at him. "You noticed first thing this morning. That was good. I am a veterinarian and I did not notice anything wrong with him yesterday either."

"He does look miserable." Alan ran his thumb along the back of the kitten's neck. From the pained look on his face, he actually looked more miserable than the poor kitten.

Quickly she went through the paces of checking the little guy's ears, nose, throat, and eyes, the same as any doctor would for any patient. It didn't take long for her diagnosis of feline coryza to be confirmed. "This little boy has a nasty respiratory infection."

"Okay." He nodded, still gently rubbing the top of the kitten's head. "Now what?"

"Now we treat him with antibiotics. Also, he's going to need to be re-hydrated. I'll set him up now with an IV and monitor him closely for the next few hours. Our biggest concern is that this does not become pneumonia. As you can imagine, little guys like this have a hard time fighting off pneumonia."

Alan swallowed hard and nodded. "But he should be okay?"

Oh, how she hated making promises. Long ago, she'd learned the hard way that things could take an unexpected turn for the worse at the drop of a hat. "Odds are in our favor. I'm very optimistic."

"That will have to do." He forced a smile.

"You should probably go home and check on the other kitty."

Alan snapped his fingers. "I forgot, the kitten is in his box in the backseat. I didn't know how long I'd be here and I didn't want to leave him alone."

"In that case, you might as will bring him in so I can check him out and make sure he's okay."

It only took a few minutes for Alan to be standing in front of her again holding up the other half of Frick and Frack.

"So far," Cindy finished her examination of the second kitty, "this fellow shows no signs of having the same thing as his brother,"

A broad smile chased away a deep sigh of relief. "Good."

"Why don't you head home. You'll have to disinfect the house because the virus stays live for at least eighteen hours. I'll want to keep this guy overnight, but I'll let you know how he's responding."

Alan's gaze drifted from her over to where the kitten was laying quietly. "If you don't mind, I'd rather stick around. At least for a little while."

All set to tell him that wasn't necessary, she realized she liked the idea of having his company. She was worried about the kitten too. "All right."

"Did you have time for breakfast this morning?"

"I'll grab a breakfast burrito out of the freezer after I'm done with this guy. You're welcome to grab one if you're hungry."

"I'm thinking you're going to need more sustenance then a breakfast burrito to get through the rest of today." He put the healthy kitty back in the box. "How about I run across the street to the diner and bring us back some real breakfast? Something that will stick to your ribs."

She hadn't heard that expression in ages, but the silent rumble in her stomach seemed to agree he had a good idea. Looking up at the clock, she figured she might have enough time to swallow a mouthful or two before her first appointment. "Make mine a western omelet with a side of bacon, and whole-grain toast with lots of extra butter. Be sure to tell Mabel it's for me. She'll get it right."

"Not worried about cholesterol, I gather." He raised one eyebrow at her.

"Try telling that one to my sister Lily. The Paris trained baker."

"Good point." He chuckled. "I'll be back shortly."

The kitten was all taken care of and resting comfortably when Alan came through the front door waving a brown paper sack in each hand. He must have the magic touch when it came to Mabel and staff. "That was fast," she mumbled quietly. She probably should have requested an iced coffee for a quick caffeine pick me up.

"Where shall I put this?"

"You choose. Inside or out?"

His gaze shifted to where the kitten was set up in a cage.

"He should be just fine for now," she reassured.

Alan nodded. "It's a lovely morning. How about outside?"

"Outside it is." She held the door open and waved an arm in the direction of the table and chairs set up on a stone patio. In another thirty minutes her staff would begin to arrive and shortly after that her day of helping the four-legged world would begin. All she had to do was keep Alan from wearing a rut in the flooring, and pray this wouldn't turn out to be one of those times when a kitten didn't get with the recovery plan.

CHAPTER TWELVE

"How do you handle the wait?" Alan stabbed at his French toast. He might be sitting outside, but his thoughts and concerns were inside with the sleeping kitty.

"It helps that in a little while this place will make a zoo look calm." She picked at a piece of bacon. "My days are pretty full, but there's always something extra. Somebody's beloved pet ate anything from a chocolate candy to a valued diamond heirloom. There will be last-minute coughs and sneezes and flus, injured limbs, or merely someone who doesn't see people very often, and myself and my staff are the only people they've spoken to in days."

"That seems kind of sad. I mean, certainly I understand if you don't want to talk to somebody, but…"

"And that's why we talk as long as the pet parent wants to."

With everything this woman had on her plate, she still took time to be kind to the lonely. Every new thing he learned about her made him realize even more what a fantastic person Hyacinth Nelson was. "How long before we'll see a change in the kitten?"

"It takes at least 24 hours to fully see the impact of antibiotics, but often I see improvements within a few hours."

"I hope so. He looked so unhappy." No matter how much he tried to shake the thought, he still felt responsible for not noticing a problem sooner.

"Who's the new kitty in the…" the pretty blonde's words trailed off

"Beth, have you met Mr. Peterson yet?" Cindy said to her tech.

Old habits kicked in. He pushed to his feet. "I'm the one who brought in the kitten."

"Nice to meet you." The young woman smiled and turned to Cindy. "Mrs. Connor called. She thinks Holly ate one of her rings."

"Thinks?"

"She said she took the ring off because it got greasy while she was eating spareribs. Now she can't find the ring. She's convinced Holly ate it."

"Is she off her food?"

Beth shook her head.

"In any pain?"

Again, Beth shook her head from side to side.

"Let me guess, we're doing an x-ray?"

"Mrs. Connor said that's what she wanted, that she wasn't going to follow the dog around all day waiting for it to expel her ring."

"Like it or not, she may have to. I am not operating on a healthy dog because she's doesn't want to start collecting poop."

"At least this way she says that she'll know if the dog ate it and what to look, or stop looking, for." Beth turned on her heel. "I'd better get back out there. I can see already it's going to be one of those days."

"I'm afraid she's right."

All Alan very much wanted to do now was reach out and wipe away all the crazy pet owners and their animal's problems. Setting his fork on the plate, he covered her hand with his.

Those bright blue eyes went from a little tired to round as saucers. "Oh, no!"

Startled, he pulled back, but not in time to avoid a collision with a squawking kamikaze. "What the…"

"Oh, Herman." Cindy jumped up and waved her arms at the feather covered mass of muscle. "Be careful, he—"

"Ouch!"

"Bites."

All he had time to do was grab at his wrist when the bird flapped its wings, almost trotted in reverse, and head forward, lunged again as Alan jumped out of the way. "I don't think he likes me."

"Herman!" Cindy shouted. "Behave yourself."

The bird actually seemed to understand her, immediately tucking his wings to his side and slowing his charge forward.

"He's a bit protective of me since I saved him after a wing injury. You might say Herman is my motivation for the wildlife center." She turned to face the bird. "You should be ashamed of yourself."

Did the goose actually bow his head with remorse? Alan rubbed at his sore arm, more fascinated with the female and goose interaction than how much his wrist hurt.

"Go find something to do." She waved at the massive grassy area behind the clinic. "Go on."

The goose squawked loudly and Alan was pretty sure shot him a dirty look before waddling away. Maybe that cozy mystery dream wasn't such a weird thing after all.

• • • •

Mortification was the only word that came to Cindy's mind. As far as Canadian geese went, Herman was mostly mild mannered. Only on occasion, when he thought someone a threat to her, did he go into scare-off-the-predator mode. At least he hadn't broken skin when he nipped at Alan.

"Maybe you should consider putting the goose in a pen." Her grandmother frowned, pulling her hand out from under the fabric and sucking on her finger. That was the third time since Cindy had stopped in that Grams had stabbed herself by mistake with the sewing needle.

"I feel so bad for him. When we try to pen him up, he gets so depressed."

Lucy stopped humming one of her favorite tunes and turned from the kitchen sink, looking over her shoulder to the cousins gathered around the island. "How can you tell a goose is depressed?"

"I don't know." Cindy shrugged. "I just know."

"How much longer before dinner is served?" Rose attempted to pilfer a pinch of Lucy's special potato salad.

A practiced hand smacked Rose's hand away. "Don't spoil your appetite."

"I'd like to leave for Boston before it gets dark. Can't I just sneak a little food now?" This time Rose tried stabbing at the salad with a fork.

The smart redhead had yet to learn, even after all these years, spoiling supper was sacrilege for Lucy. Not only did she smack Rose's hand away, she moved the bowl out of reach.

"You're leaving us so soon, dear?" Grams looked up from her quilting.

Rose stole a grape from the fruit bowl. "According to my office, the exhibit has finally cleared all obstacles and will be on our doorstep bright and early tomorrow morning. If it is not, I will personally go down there and load and haul the thing myself."

"If they know what's good for them," Poppy sneaked around Lucy and snatched a piece of Canadian bacon, "it will get delivered on time."

"I saw that," Lucy called out without looking up.

Sporting an impish grin, Poppy gave her cousin a quiet high five.

"Heard that too." Despite the grumpy reprove, anyone who knew the family housekeeper could hear the amusement in her voice.

"Is Alan joining us for dinner?" Rose asked

"Nope." Cindy reached for a handful of grapes. "He wants to stay home with the other kitten. As a matter of fact, he insisted on feeding me, since I won't charge him for taking care of the kitten."

"How is the poor baby?" Grams managed to insert the needle and retrieve it without stabbing herself.

"Much better. The antibiotics seem to be helping. He's much more comfortable, and he's even drinking on his own. I debated whether to take him home tonight or not, but we had a couple of surgeries today. Since I had to call in help for a night shift anyhow, this way he can be monitored regularly a little longer."

"I hope you can still bring Alan to the art auction Thursday night." Rose slid onto a seat beside her.

Slamming the fridge door shut, Poppy poured herself a glass of juice. "Who does a fundraiser on a Thursday night?"

"Obviously," Rose scowled at her cousin, "we do. Believe it or not we have a better turnout midweek than we do on weekends. Probably because we're not competing with every other gallery, museum, or charity in the city of Boston."

"Or," Cindy added, "every socialite's birthday or anniversary."

"See, she gets it." Rose pointed to her cousin. "So, is he coming?"

"I didn't even say I was coming."

"Don't be silly. Close the clinic early, it's just a few hours drive.

You can enjoy free food and drink. All it will cost you are some smiles and laughs at the right people. I'll introduce you to all the important donors so you don't waste your time chatting up a dud, and Herman will be closer to having a pen-free place to roam without anyone getting bitten."

She had to admit she liked the idea of tapping people outside of Lawford Mountain. And Boston did offer an awful lot of people with capital to spare.

"I can see the twinkle in her eye." Poppy smiled. "She's in."

"Yeah, I think I am, but I don't know about Alan. I mean, up until recently, he was a bit of a hermit. I don't think the social scene is any more his thing than it is mine."

"That's what Rose is good at." A platter of marinated meat in her hands, Lucy paused at the back door. "You just let her do her thing. You'll see it will all work out." The woman flashed a bright grin and marched outside singing the title song from her favorite musical.

"I'll give you a hand with the grill. My fingers need the rest." Grams smiled and followed Lucy out the door, humming the same tune.

"Uh, oh." Her hand halfway to her mouth, Poppy dropped the grape and swung on her stool to face her cousins. "Did she invite someone else to dinner?"

The same concern that plagued Poppy struck Cindy. Lucy loved to hum and sing tunes from her favorite show, but whenever she sang "Hello Dolly" out loud with the energy of a Broadway singer on stage, the woman was cooking up a scheme. And that didn't bode well for someone.

"Don't worry." Callie came in the doorway. "It's not us."

"Not that I'm worried. I'm leaving town after dinner." Rose gave her cousin a hug. "But you look awfully sure of yourself."

"I am."

"Okay." Cindy waved her hands at her sister. "What don't we know?"

"I just ran into Bobby from the marina at the One Stop. He got a phone call while I was there."

Cindy didn't have a clue where this was going.

"From Lucy." Head in the fridge, Callie paused to pour herself a drink. "She's been chatting up the guest in the Elm cottage. The one whose buddy got stuck at work and is showing up a couple of days late for their fishing trip."

Anticipation building, everyone in the room nodded.

"And you know how the gal in the Birch cabin is there alone because her boyfriend dumped her over the phone for her best friend?"

"I can't believe people really do such sleazy things." Maybe it was because she worked for a church, or maybe that she was the baby of the family, but Poppy always saw life as though it were a retro sitcom.

"What no one probably knows," Callie continued, "is that Lucy just happened to mention there's a carnival in town in Billings this week and since neither had anything to do today they should borrow the General's jeep and check it out."

"I don't remember hearing that." Cindy frowned.

"Probably because the carnival is coming to Billings next month," Poppy reminded her.

"So they had to drive there and back together, but what does Bobby have to do with any of it?"

Callie set her glass down. "Lucy forgot to mention that the gas meter is broken and a full tank may not be full."

"Oh, no. She didn't suggest they use the short cut through Beaver's Pass?" Rose waved her hand after three pairs of eyes bore into her. "Never mind. Of course she did. With the lousy cell reception around here, those poor folks could be stuck for days if no one goes looking."

"Exactly." Callie nodded. "Lucy thought Bobby should go rescue them before dark."

"Well, maybe this time it'll work out." Poppy bit into another grape.

Callie smiled sweetly at her sister. Too sweetly. "Did I mention who else I ran into?"

"And the other shoe dangles menacingly." Rose lowered her voice from deep in her throat.

"At the suggestion of Mr. Elm Cabin's buddy, his fiancé is here to surprise him until the buddy can get free."

A choral groan filled the room.

"And the other shoe falls with a boom." Cindy slid off the chair and stood. "On that note, I'm going to head out and check on kitten number two."

Amongst a few more jokes and hugging Rose goodbye, Cindy wondered on her way to Alan's how any one woman with her lousy track record had not yet given up on channeling Dolly Levi. On the other hand, odds had to be in Lucy's favor that one of these days she would get a match right.

All the cabins came equipped with a small outdoor grill. For some reason she had expected dinner at Alan's to be take out from one of the local restaurants. She hadn't expected to find him on the porch actually cooking.

At the sound of her car door slamming, he closed the cover and met her at the porch stairs. "I hope you like steak."

"Medium, if you don't mind."

"A woman after my own heart."

"How's the kitten doing?" She followed him onto the porch and into the house. The object of her question came trotting up to her. "Well, hi there."

Alan scooped him into his arms. "I think he's missing his brother. He's been meowing much more than usual today."

"I'm not surprised." She retrieved the fur ball from his arms and examined more closely. "He could still come down with something, but so far he looks pretty good. We might have dodged a bullet with this one."

"I'll feel better when they are together again." Leading the way into the kitchen, he opened the cupboards and took out two glasses. "Is red wine okay?"

She nodded. "Perfect."

"Do you think the kittens will be adopted together?" He poured the wine.

"We will certainly try." Even though it was important in her job that she not get attached to orphaned animals, she'd already decided that if he didn't keep them, she wanted them. Probably her odd way of staying close to him.

"Do you like your salad with your steak or before?"

"With is fine."

He handed her a glass, and placing his hand on her back, nudged her toward the living room. "It's almost chilly enough to start a fire."

Taking a seat on the well-worn sofa, she noticed one side of the table was set for dinner for two, but the other side was almost completely cleared of his usual paperwork and clutter. A glaring reminder that his time here was almost over.

"I was thinking." He put his drink down on the coffee table. "Are you going to attend the museum fundraiser?"

"As a matter of fact, yes."

Twisting to face her, he plastered on a sweet smile. "If the invitation is still open, I'd like to join you."

"Really?"

He nodded.

"I didn't think you would like that sort of thing."

"I don't. Usually."

"Then why? Doing the street fair is more than enough."

"But if I can do more to help Herman find a home with other geese…"

Cindy tried not to laugh. "Did we traumatize you?"

"Of course not. I plot murder and mayhem for a living." He chuckled. "But it made me see why you are so passionate about the sanctuary. The two kittens, the goose, the fox on the road. It's a good thing that you want to do. And I want to help."

The way his eyes almost pleaded for her to agree made her heart do a little back flip and then melt in her chest. All she could do was nod. She had no idea what her heart was going to do when this book was finished and he returned to his life clear across the country.

CHAPTER THIRTEEN

"Don't you two look precious." Lucy clapped her hands together then scooped the kittens up.

"Oh, my." Fiona Hart came out from the kitchen. "What have we here?"

Snuggling the two kitties against her chest, Lucy turned to Grams. "We're babysitting."

"Number One has only been home for two days, and even though he's doing very well, I'm concerned about leaving them alone." Alan reached out and scratched the kittens head. "Not to mention, he needs his antibiotics."

"Number One?" Cindy's grandmother asked.

"Since his return from the clinic I've been calling them Number One and Number Two."

"Oh, we're going to have to do better than that." The graceful older woman lifted one of the kittens up to her face and rubbed her nose against it. "Don't you worry. Lucy is an expert at medicating kitties."

Alan actually had to smother a smile with his hand when Lucy's brows shot high on her forehead at Mrs. Hart's words.

"Here she comes." Mrs. Hart turned her attention to the massive staircase and Alan did his best not to swallow his tongue.

Every chance he'd had to spend time with Cindy, she'd been wearing her standard attire of jeans or khakis, and a button down polo shirt. Now, in an off the shoulder, formfitting dress, almost the same dark blue shade as her eyes, she looked stunning. "Hi."

"Sorry, I'm running a little late." In heels just high enough to show of the shapeliness of her legs, she trotted down the stairs the same way she might have if she were in running shoes and gym shorts. At the bottom she extended her arm, dangling a necklace at her grandmother. "This is perfect, Grams. I just didn't have anything nice enough at home. Thank you, but I'm going to need help, please."

"Alan, would you mind?" Her grandmother pointed to the kitten with her chin. "We have our hands full."

"Oh, of course not." He took the necklace and moved to stand behind Cindy. His knuckles brushed gently across her shoulders and he heard her breath hitch in sync with his own. Slipping the hook into the clasp, he snapped the safety catch and took a step in retreat. "There you go."

"I think we're all set. We should be able to hit Boston before traffic gets too horrific." She turned to kiss her Grams and Lucy. "We'll sell this idea to the investors and then head back, but we'll still be back late."

There was no doubt in his mind this woman could do anything she put her mind to and excel at it. Not many women could go from country enthusiast to fundraising society matron in the blink of an eye. But Hyacinth Nelson was not just any woman.

"You should stay in town with Rose. We can handle the kittens overnight," her grandmother reassured.

"I know, Grams, but I have to be at work bright and early and Alan still has a book to finish."

He hadn't mentioned to her that he'd finished the book last night. Despite the time he'd lost worrying about Number One, ever since Cindy came into his life the words had flowed almost non-stop. And as much as he could argue it was the landscape and the people, he knew it was one *people*. Hyacinth.

"Shall we go?" Extending his elbow, he offered his arm and knew no matter who else was at this evening's little soiree, he would be the envy of every man in the place.

● ● ● ●

"Wow. I should have known this place, and Rose, would put on a five-star event." Cindy was delighted she'd listened to her grandmother and dressed up a few notches for the midweek event. Spending most of her life on the mountain, she'd forgotten how different the rest of the world could be.

"In the little time I have spent with your family, if I have learned one thing, it is that not a single one of you does anything less than five-star."

"Thank you." It might not have been necessary to hang on to Alan's arm any longer, but she needed a few more minutes to get her bearings.

"Toto, I don't think we're in Kansas anymore," she muttered out of one side of her mouth.

Alan laughed hard and loud and didn't even flinch at all the heads that turned in their direction. They were most definitely not in Lawford anymore. Not that she hadn't figured that out the minute they'd hit city traffic. Still, this was her first visit to the museum since Rose had been associated with it, and her first time ever mingling with the exclusive patrons and not as a paying visitor. She'd be lying if she didn't admit, all dressed up or not, she was a little bit nervous.

"You okay?" He squeezed her hand.

"Of course." All see needed to see was his slanted glance under raised brows to know he didn't believe her. "Is it that obvious?"

"Only to me. You're cutting off the circulation in my arm."

"Oh." She loosened her grip. "I'm sorry."

"Don't be." He did his best to flash a reassuring smile. "I'm a little nervous myself."

The smile worked. Tension slid away and a tiny laugh bubbled up. "Don't we make quite the pair."

"There you are!" Much like her grandmother, Rose practically glided across the exhibit room and slid her hand into Alan's free elbow. "I've been telling everyone about you."

"Me?" he muttered. "This is about Cindy and the wildlife center."

"Yes, but you are the bait."

"I don't think I like the sound of that," Cindy mumbled so only Alan could hear. Even if her cousin did have a point, did she have to be so blunt about it?

"Rose, darling." A tall blonde dripping in diamonds sauntered over and kissed the air by Rose's cheek. "What a lovely job you've done. The exhibit is just exquisite."

"And we wouldn't be able to accomplish it without donors like you and Mr. Rockford. We're so glad you could join us for this little celebratory fete."

"We try to do our part." The woman had a contrite smile down pat.

A gentleman, who Cindy assumed was Mr. Rockford, sidled up beside Mrs. Rockford and handed her a glass of champagne. "Have a glass, Marjorie. It's not a bad year."

"I'm not surprised." The blonde accepted the flute. "Remember Rose Preston? Rebecca and Ted's daughter."

"Of course." While it was possible with a little coaxing he might remember who Aunt Becky and Uncle Ted were, Cindy was pretty sure at this particular moment the guy didn't have the slightest recall of Rose.

Standing awkwardly beside her, Alan leaned in and whispered, "If you'll excuse me a minute, I think I'm going to find us some of that liquid courage."

Cindy nodded.

"Oh, you must excuse me a moment." Rose spoke to the Rockford's but her gaze focused clear across the room. "There's someone I need to speak with."

If she'd yanked any harder, Rose would have pulled Cindy's shoulder out of its socket. Not till they were halfway across the room did her cousin slow her steps and notice Alan was not with them. "Where did he go?"

"In search of courage."

Rose halted long enough to frown at her cousin.

"He'll probably be looking for us any second now."

The creases on her forehead eased and the well practiced smile was back in place. "Well, he'll have to find us over here. We've only got a couple of hours to work on a handful of key people and we might as well start now."

Might as well. The family was right. Their sweet Rose was actually very good at living in both worlds.

It took a few moments for Cindy to realize her cousin was gunning for the guy who looked to belong on both the cover of a fortune five hundred magazine as well as *GQ*. And of course, he had a pretty young blonde at his side. What she couldn't decide was if it was his daughter, his wife, or just a friend.

"Edgar." Something in the tone of Rose's voice gave Cindy the impression that Rose knew the man as someone other than a name on a guest list.

"Rose." Greeting Rose with a casual hug, he had the good manners to immediately introduce his companion. "Have you met Abigail Larabey?"

"I can't say that I've had the pleasure." Rose extended her hand and Cindy thanked her lucky stars that she did not have to brown nose rich people for a living.

For the next few moments, casual greetings and compliments were exchanged. Cindy did her best to keep up with the conversation, smile politely on cue, and nod whenever her input was appropriate. Two of the things her grandfather had made a point to remind her would be important tonight if she wanted to actually get some money out of the old fogies was to, one: keep her eyes on the donor; and two: always offer up a strong handshake. Both came rushing to mind. From the snippets of banter tossed about she'd been able to glean that the arm candy was just that. Neither wife, nor official girlfriend, the attractive lady obviously fell into the character of *friend*.

By the time the conversation shifted to Mucky Muck's latest acquisitions, Cindy had become distracted searching for Alan. Where had he gone to for that liquid courage—France?

"I thought you were a fan." Rose smiled and Cindy realized she had no idea what direction the conversation had taken. The only thing she was pretty sure of is that this guy was most likely a fan of Alan, because other than Herman, no one else within a 200 mile radius would have a clue who she was.

Rose must have said something else to him, because Mr. Mucky Muck had stepped into her private space and smiled down at her as though she held the secret of the golden goose. "Tell me more," he said coolly.

Oh hell, she really should have paid more attention to the conversation. Alan was a big boy and could take care of himself. Most likely some other person had waylaid him for an autograph or some such fan thing.

Rose waited a beat and just as Cindy was about to apologize for not paying attention, her cousin stepped in to save her. "Cindy can explain so much more to you about the need for caring for our wildlife and educating our youth. How is the fox?"

Fox? Who told Rose about the fox? "Last time we saw her and her pup she was happily reunited with the father and siblings."

"Really?" Mucky Muck actually looked interested.

"Yes, and according to a local business owner who we believe is situated near the den, she's seen the family since and Mama looks just fine."

"But you need more help?" he asked with more sincerity than she'd anticipated.

"Yes. I'm—"

"Excuse me." Turning slightly away from Mr. Mucky Muck, Rose tapped her on the arm and winked. "I'd better make the rounds before my boss accuses me of playing favorites."

"And I'm going to see where the waiters went with those delicious shrimp bruschetta," the blonde that had been hanging on like an extra appendage announced.

Mr. Mucky Muck barely nodded at her. Cindy was rather surprised to find she had his undivided attention. Rose really knew how to pick them.

"So, you were saying?" he urged her on.

"Part of the problem is that I'm not a wildlife specialist. I can tend to the occasional mishap, but if I'd found an orphaned fawn or fox pup, those would have to be taught to live in the wild and properly returned to their habitat. I have neither the time nor the skill set to take on chores like that. While we have been blessed with a wonderful volunteer system—"

"Like a volunteer fire department," he interjected.

She smiled. "Yes, I suppose so, but still, we need full time professional assistance. An education center would go a long way to help sustain the remainder of the center."

"And Rose tells me that you already have a donation of some land?"

"That's right. A generous donation, but construction for the facility isn't going to be cheap."

"No." He shook his head and smiled at her. "Never is."

"Do you like geese?"

"Geese?" He seemed surprised by her question.

"Canadian Geese. They're a protected species but can be a challenge."

"Really?"

She supposed all he knew about geese was *fois gras*, but she proceeded to tell him about how she found and treated Herman and now because he could no longer fly, he'd more or less become the clinic mascot. From the corner of her eye she'd spotted Alan across the room. Sure enough, two champagne flutes in hand, he'd barely managed to edge away from one very talkative gentleman, only to be stopped by another person.

Except this time, the person was decidedly feminine, well dressed, rather attractive, and the way her hand settled unmoving on his arm and her gaze locked to his seemed a tad too possessive. "What the heck?"

"Excuse me?" Mucky Muck asked.

"Sorry, where was I?"

"Herman."

"Oh, yes." Halfway through how it would only be fair to Herman if he could be placed in a sanctuary with other rehabilitated geese, she noticed yet another woman approach Alan. This one threw her arms around him in a warm embrace and Cindy clamped her mouth shut, counted to ten, and reminded herself she had no claim on Alan Peterson.

Then again, maybe it was time she did something about that.

CHAPTER FOURTEEN

Never had detouring for two drinks been such an obstacle course. Rose had prepped her attendees well. Alan suspected that even those who were not fans of his work were at least enthusiastic about a photo-op with a bestselling author. Of course it didn't hurt his reputation any that two of his recent releases had been quickly turned into big screen blockbusters.

Across the room he spotted Cindy and Rose accompanied by a couple. Except, from where he stood, he could see that the male half of the duo was sizing Cindy up. Any red-blooded male would have recognized the predatory glint in the guy's eye. A glint that brought out every protective instinct Alan had, and an irresistible urge to mark his turf. Except Cindy wasn't his turf. *Blast.*

"Well isn't this the last place I'd expect to find you."

Alan turned to the familiar voice. "Margaret. How nice to see you."

"I bet." The always classically dressed woman laid a hand on his forearm and smiled up at him. "I didn't realize you'd abandoned the California sunshine for true civilization."

If his former publisher knew he'd spent the last month about as far away from civilization as possible without actually pitching a tent in Big Foot's backyard, she'd have asked him what he'd been smoking. "Does this mean you've given up on New York?"

"Not at all—"

"Alan!" Another more familiar voice squealed from behind seconds before a pair of feminine arms flew around him. "Why didn't you tell me you were coming to Boston?"

"Amanda." This little party was most definitely filled with surprises. "How long have you been in Boston?"

Her hand smacked his side. "You know my family has a house on the Cape. This time of year, there's nowhere else to find me."

"There you are." Stealing one of the glasses, Rose smiled at the crowd and clutched his now free hand. "I was about to send out search and rescue."

"Sorry about that." Especially since he didn't like the idea of Cindy alone with Mr. Perfect.

Margaret casually glanced at the nametag Rose wore, alerting all to her museum affiliation. "The museum has outdone itself this evening."

"Thank you." Rose beamed, exchanged a few more polite words then lifted the glass she'd pilfered from him in the direction of where Cindy and company stood. "If you'll excuse us, I have a few more people to introduce Mr. Peters to."

"Of course." Margaret sidestepped him, leaning in. "Call me while you're in town. We'll do lunch."

"Only in town for this little shindig and then heading back to my writing cave."

"Too bad," Margaret purred. "Maybe next time."

As he turned to follow Rose practically dragging him away, he nodded at Margaret.

"I'll join you." Thanks to Amanda latching onto his other arm, champagne sloshed over the rim of his glass. "Oops."

With Amanda hanging on him from one side and Rose tugging from the other, Alan had a new appreciation for the rope in tug of war. If luck was on his side he wouldn't snap in two.

"Here you go." Rose handed Cindy the champagne glass she'd taken from him. "I hope you two found plenty to chat about?"

Mr. Perfect bobbed his head. "This new project sounds very worthwhile."

"Oh, it is. Mr. Peters here is going to be involved in the fundraising as well." Rose gestured in Alan's direction. "Have I introduced you yet to Alan Peters?"

Perfect's eyes rounded for an instant before a calm façade of indifference took over. "The author?"

Alan nodded. "That would be me."

"I've read your books." Perfect seemed to have, thankfully, lost interest in Cindy. Already Alan knew one thing for sure about this guy. He was an idiot.

"That's always nice to hear." In all the years since Alan had first bumped into a fan, he'd never quite mastered how to respond.

"He's very good," Amanda offered, still hanging onto his arm.

Perfect's gaze bounced momentarily in Amanda's direction.

"I'm sorry," Alan shifted his weight in a vain effort to escape her grasp. "This is Amanda."

"Amanda Peterson." She extended her hand.

"It's a pleasure," Mr. Perfect said.

But there was no missing how Cindy's eyes sparked with surprise.

"My brother Glenn's wife," he explained quickly

Amanda grinned up at him, and to his chagrin, tightened her hold. "Ex-wife."

● ● ● ●

A myriad of things ran through Cindy's mind, not the least of which was that Amanda had way too tight a grip on her brother-in-law's arm. Ex or not.

For a moment, Rose's gaze flickered with annoyance at Alan's ex sister-in-law before she turned her attention back to the Mucky Muck. "Alan is scheduled to do a book signing in Lawford and is donating some of the proceeds to the wildlife project."

"Oh, really?" His eyes sparked with interest. "When will this be?"

"Next weekend," Cindy responded, redirecting her attention to the man with the money. "The signing is actually part of a much bigger street fair." For the first time since Alan joined the conversation, Mucky Muck's attention returned to Cindy. Not that she cared. All she wanted were more non-resident donations and she didn't care if that came from a love of mystery books, or wildlife, or small towns, but the glint of interest in his eyes had her rambling on. "There will be everything from a petting zoo and face painting for the children to the sidewalk sale and food trucks for adults." If nothing else, if his stomach was the way to a man's heart, one could easily adjust that to be food is the way to a man's wallet.

"And don't forget the music," Rose chimed in. "And of course there will be more of these lovely desserts. Have you been to the dessert tables?"

"As a matter of fact, I have. The shrimp bruschettas are excellent and those cheese balls were exquisite—"

"Actually, that's our vegan option. They're quinoa balls."

"Well, they're addictive, but not nearly as much as the dessert section. I think I've tried one of everything at least twice."

"The sweet selection comes from my sister's bakery." Cindy couldn't stop herself from grinning proudly over Lily's accomplishments. "She owns the Pastry Stop in Lawford."

"I've heard of it."

He had? Wow. Now Cindy really wanted to grin at her sister's accomplishments in such a short time.

"Now I understand why everyone gives the place such rave reviews." His gaze shifted to Cindy. "I may have to make the time to visit in person."

The intensity of his gaze almost had her taking a step back. This wouldn't be the first time a man had paid her extra attention, and this *was* all for a good cause. "We'd love to have you. Are you busy next weekend?"

Mucky seemed startled by the question, or perhaps intrigued, but slowly his lips tipped north and his eyes twinkled at her. "Nothing I can't change."

"Perhaps," Rose said casually, looking at Alan, "we could offer large donors a special private event with Mr. Peters."

It took Alan a few moments to realize that was not a conjecture but a suggestion awaiting his response. "I think that could definitely be arranged. What did you have in mind?"

Without taking time to think, Rose volleyed back, "Perhaps a pre-festivities brunch?" When no one responded, she pressed on. "At the lake away from the strolling tourists." This time Mucky's head motioned slightly up and down.

"We can have Lily make her *apfel* kuchen," Cindy chimed in, hoping to appeal to the man's sense of exclusive privilege. "The dessert she doesn't sell at the shop. It's only for family and close friends."

Mucky's eyebrows inched slowly up into his hairline. Even Amanda eased her grip on Alan and leaned in closer to Cindy.

Apparently he wasn't the only one with a sweet tooth.

"How much?" Mucky directed at Rose.

Still smiling, her cousin straightened her five foot seven frame to level her gaze into the over six foot tall Mr. Mucky's eyes. "Strong five."

He nodded. "How many donors?"

Instead of the quick response, Rose hesitated a moment, and then, lips that had been pressed tightly together in thought, blurted out, "Top five. That will make a round table for six just the right size."

A smile that could have won a national election for the guy bloomed across his face. With a curt nod of his head, she had her first serious donor. Later she'd have to ask Rose for how much since she wasn't completely sure what had just been exchanged and didn't think asking was considered good form.

"If you will excuse me," leaning closer to Cindy so no one else could see, Rose winked, "I have a few more people to introduce Mr. Peters to."

"I'd best make the rounds myself." Mucky smiled down at her. "I look forward to seeing you next weekend."

Cindy nodded. She had a feeling she might be doing that a lot the rest of the evening. Especially if Rose managed to use Alan and Lily's baked goods to charm all of the patrons that easily.

"So your sister baked all these delicious sweets?"

Still stunned that she had a major donor for her wildlife project, she'd forgotten that she'd been left alone with clingy Amanda. "Yes. She runs the Pastry Stop in Lawford."

"Well. There's one little cookie here that I can't seem to resist and my waistline is no doubt going to make me pay for it." Amanda held up a spitzbuben. Didn't matter, so many of the things Lily baked were addictive. "Too bad I already have plans for next weekend."

Doing an actual fist pump instead of a mental one was probably another thing that would not be in good form. Instead, Cindy smiled and glanced across the room to Rose working a circle of women and poor Alan standing in the midst, nodding and smiling. Even though he seemed perfectly at ease, she could see the stiffness in his stance. She really owed this sweet guy. And so would all the animals that the new center would help.

"You really like him." Again, Amanda caught her off guard.

"I'm sorry. I was distracted. What was that?"

Amanda's gaze darted from Cindy to where interested donors were currently swarming around Alan and back again. She swallowed a muffled laugh and shook her head. "For what it's worth, he's a nice guy. Always has been. Did you know we actually dated a few times?"

She shook her head. In the grand scheme of things, she knew very little about Alan Peterson.

"That's how I met his brother." Rolling her eyes, she bit back a self-deprecating grunt. "I let my ex's good looks sway me."

What was wrong with Alan's looks?

"My mother always said stay away from the charmers. Did I listen? Noooo."

Alan could be charming. Look at him now. Even out of his comfort zone, he had all the women eating out of his hand.

"But," she sighed, "*c'est la vie*. You're probably a better fit for him anyhow."

What? Her gaze shot up and over to Alan again.

"Oh, yeah." Amanda nodded. "I'm not up for a cat fight."

"Cat fight?"

"If you want him that bad, honey, he's all yours. Besides, it's obvious to any idiot the feeling is mutual."

It is? Her mind replayed the last conversation with Rose and Mr. Mucky Muck. What had Amanda seen?

"Well," Amanda opened her small purse and rummaged through, "I'm sure the festival will be a huge success for your cause." She pulled out a checkbook and pen and scribbled on it. "Though the museum may not be happy the animals just got their donation."

A check dangled in front of her and Cindy felt her heart skip a beat at the sight of the numbers.

"Just fill out whoever it goes to." She patted Cindy on the arm. "I have to run. Be good to him, cause if you're not, I'll be back and next time I won't give up so easily."

Cindy stared down at the check. Her cousin had been right, coming here had been the smart thing to do. Not just for the money, but for Alan. Amanda had been right too. Alan and her were a good fit. A fit that deserved more time. Now she just had to make him see that. But how?

CHAPTER FIFTEEN

"**I** can't believe *anyone* would pay sixty thousand dollars to have brunch with me." The entire concept boggled Alan's mind.

"*Five* anyones."

"Well. Not all five paid that."

"No, but close enough." Cindy shifted the car into a higher gear and took off on the finally clear highway. "What I don't understand is how anyone can live in the city like that. I think there are more cars in Boston than people in all of New England."

"Every big city has its own charm, but you're probably right about the cars."

"I'm sure of it, and for the record, if I had it, I would."

"Live in Boston?"

"Lord, no. I'm a country girl through and through."

That thought made him smile. She really was. It was only one of the things he loved about her. *Loved.* He almost laughed at himself. Somehow in little more than a week he'd finished the book from hell, become a cat person, and fallen in love. Go figure.

"I meant," she continued, "if I had sixty thousand dollars, I'd spend it to have brunch with you."

"Fortunately for you, I come at a bargain price for friends and family." All he had to figure out was how to sell himself to her as more than a seasonal friend of the family.

"I suppose that's a good thing because I don't have an abundance of cash floating around."

He smiled and slid down slightly, leaning against the head rest. "The roads really are beautiful up here. As beautiful as the West Coast is, it's a totally different vibe."

"You should see it in the fall. The kaleidoscope of colors, the oranges, yellows, and reds are absolutely magnificent. I'm always so thankful that tourists spend a fortune to come and see the foliage in hopes of hitting during the right season and we get a front row seat for free."

He liked that idea. A front row seat. Not just to the fall foliage, but to everything that happened around here. As far as small towns went, living in Lawford wasn't anything like the archaic civilization he'd imagined when his grandfather had talked him into coming here to finish his book. People were nice. Friendly. Everybody cared about everybody. The smaller shops were more accommodating than any large box store. There were indeed a few quirky things. Floyd's barber shop was an interesting tale to tell. The General was certainly a colorful patriarch. Though Mrs. Hart was nothing like his own grandmother. Alan would have expected a by the book hard-nosed general to be married to a woman nearly as regimented and orderly as he must have been. Or perhaps, the polarity of their personalities explained why the relationship survived decades longer than that of his grandparents. And of course the Merry Widows club had a gaggle of interesting characters. But none of it mattered as much as the lovely veterinarian with a heart of gold and spine of steel. "We made a good team tonight."

"Yeah." She tapped her long fingers on the steering wheel. "We did. Though Rose really is the one who made it happen."

"That girl is wasting talent working with historical *objects d'art.*"

"I can't decide if she should be a party planner or a fundraiser, because she does both very well."

"She certainly knows how to work a room. Not only do we have the five donors for brunch at the lake, but she got pledges from others in the room for almost $100,000 more."

Keeping her eyes on the road, Cindy fished into the handbag at her side and pulled out a folded piece of paper. "Your friend gave me this."

His friend? He unfolded the paper, immediately recognizing the name. "$5000. If I didn't know any better I'd say she has a guilty conscience."

"Really?"

Alan placed the check lightly on her purse again. "Let's just say my brother did not live up to her expectations, and Amanda is not one to hang onto anything that doesn't improve her prospects in life."

"I'm sorry."

"We all are. Some people are simply never happy with what they have."

Cindy nodded. "I've met my share of those."

"Now I'm the one who's sorry."

She shook her head. "Don't be. At least I didn't marry him."

Suddenly Alan had an irresistible urge to break the neck of a man he'd never known. On the other hand, he should probably thank the character for having screwed up enough that Alan was now here in the company of this special woman and not the character.

"Traffic is really light." Cindy turned off the highway and onto the main drag that would take them straight to Lawford and Hart Land.

"Wow. That went fast."

"Always feels that way going home. I took every science class imaginable under the sun and have never figured out why that is."

Alan had a pretty good idea that this evening, the reason had nothing to do with science or traffic, but the company. He'd enjoyed every minute of conversation, and his view of his date. Not that she'd considered it a date, but he liked the sound of it. "Would you think me silly if I said I wonder how the kittens are doing?"

Cindy laughed. "I'm sure they're fine, but we'll be home soon. You can see for yourself then."

Home. Oh, he really liked the way that word rolled off her tongue. Maybe it wasn't their home, or even his home, but still, the sound of it coming from Cindy held an irresistible appeal. And wasn't that seriously nice.

• • • •

"How long did we stand tonight?" Her shoes dangling from her fingers, Cindy walked barefoot toward Hart House. "Somebody needs to invent black-tie sneakers."

"They have." Alan stretched out his arm and snatched her hand in his. "I saw them at a wedding. Keds covered in silver sequins."

"Now you tell me." With every step, she waited for him to pull back his hand. By the time they reached the porch, she realized he had no intention of letting go and her heart did a little jig. His earlier comment about their making a good team replayed in her mind. She'd liked it when he'd said it in the car, and she loved it now even more.

Much to her surprise, the General and company were still on the porch playing cards. Then again, all night card games were nothing new at the lake, and she suspected, tonight in particular, everyone had to be curious how the evening had gone.

"Oh, good. You're home. Tell us, how did it go?" Grams must've been filling in at the card table for somebody. "Did you make some connections?"

Alan squeezed her hand, but didn't let go. Instead, he grinned at her, waiting for her to share the good news.

"You could say that. We have over $300,000 in pledges."

"Oh, my sweet Lord." Grams dropped her cards.

"Fiona, dear." For the first time that she could remember, appalled, the General turned at his wife. "Your cards, dear, we can see your cards."

The woman casually waved her husband off, pushed to her feet, and hurried up to Cindy. "Did I hear you correctly?"

Cindy bobbed her head. "Yes. There's something else though."

"That doesn't sound good." Ralph scooped up the cards from the table.

"What in blue blazes are you doing?" The General looked at Ralph.

Ralph rolled his eyes. "We all know what Fiona's holding, and right now nobody cares about the cards. We all want to hear about the money."

"That's right, dear." Fiona momentarily flashed her husband a smile before returning her attention to her granddaughter. "What else is there?"

"We can expect five donors for brunch on Saturday with Alan."

All heads turned to Alan.

"Heavy donors," he added.

"Very heavy donors." At least as far as Cindy was concerned, strong five, which she now understood to mean high five figures, was plenty heavy.

"I heard you pull up." Lucy appeared with a box and Alan's kittens. And no matter what the man claimed, they were his kittens. "They were perfectly well behaved, and absolutely adorable."

"They look like the lot under the willow cabin," Ralph mentioned, leaning over to scratch one behind the ear.

"Yes." The General cleared his throat. "Tell us more about this brunch."

While Alan retrieved the kittens, carefully checking each one out and taking a minute to love on one, then the other, Cindy filled everyone in on how the evening had gone and all the donations. She did, however, leave out Alan's ex sister-in-law and her check. Why spoil the evening's fun?

"I think it's all marvelous." Louise pushed to her feet. "And past my bedtime."

"I'll join you." Thelma stood and stretched left then right. "So glad all went well. We knew you could do it."

Ralph raised a brow at Thelma and Cindy wondered what that was all about.

"All right." Thelma sighed. "Maybe Ralph knew you'd do better than I did."

Louise cleared her throat.

"Fine. So I came in a little low," Thelma huffed.

"A little?" Ralph teased.

"Wait a minute." Cindy raised her free hand. "What is going on?"

Lucy let out a low chuckle. "Everyone's got a ten spot on how much money you'd raise."

"You bet on me!" Cindy couldn't believe it.

"Well," Lucy shrugged, "technically on both of you."

Alan smothered a laugh, and Cindy couldn't decide if she should be pleased or offended. "So who won?"

Their summer neighbor since Cindy's childhood, Ralph flashed a toothy grin at her. "I may not have won, but I had you in for $500,000. You came close."

That surprised the heck out of her. Maybe she'd been living in the country too long, but it simply hadn't occurred to her that art patrons would be willing to drop that much money at a museum and have so much left over to save animals.

"I won." Lucy handed Alan the box. "I may have shortchanged you a bit, but at $255,000, I was closest."

"That's only because I placed my bet on two fifty before you placed yours." Louise turned to Cindy. "Not that it matters of course. What's important is that you raised money for the poor animals."

Holding the screen door open, Thelma nodded. "That's right, all that matters is that you accomplished what you set out to do."

"That's right." Louise nodded at her friend.

A few feet behind her, Ralph stopped, shook his head at Cindy, and softly mouthed, "Fifty k. The woman is an underachiever," and marched out the door.

Cindy almost laughed. If she'd known about the pool, she wouldn't have gone much higher than ten k herself.

"Well," Alan stood awkwardly by the door, "I should go too. Settle these guys in for the night."

Cindy nodded. "I also need to get home. I have patients bright and early tomorrow."

"Night dear." Grams hugged her. "And good job."

"Thanks." Still smiling, she followed Alan outside and walking slowly, noticed the porch light turn off. Everyone had gone inside. "Thanks for coming, and helping. And, well, everything."

He set the box down on the hood of his rental car and snatched her hand as he'd done earlier, threading his fingers in hers. "It was very much my pleasure."

One of the kittens must have shifted, making the box move.

"You'd better get them home before they wake up and want to play." As much as she'd rather stand here under the moonlight, holding hands with him, somewhere in her veterinarian's oath it must have mentioned to put sleeping kitties before anything she might want.

"Mm," he mumbled, then leaned in for a goodnight kiss.

The feel of his lips on hers made her forget all about the kittens, the mountain's wildlife, the card games, and the bets. Her hand slid up his shoulder and around his neck. This was most definitely where she wanted to be.

The box shifted and bumped into Cindy's hip seconds before a paw batted at her.

"So, this is what parenthood is like?" Alan released his hold on her and nudged the kitten back into the box. "I should go."

She nodded. Words weren't forming yet in her fogged mind.

"But I want a rain check."

She nodded again. So did she.

CHAPTER SIXTEEN

The big day had finally arrived. Cindy was so nervous anyone would think her entire life depended on the success of the first annual Lawford Street Fair.

"Here you go." Lily set another pie on the counter. "Okay, these are the last to be delivered. They go to Betty's Cut and Curl. She's already got the table set up."

"Good thing too. Louise texted me an hour ago that early arrivals are already walking along and shopping."

"I know." Lily smiled. "Mabel put in a last minute order for extra cupcakes. Becky is putting them in the oven now."

"But the fair doesn't officially start for a couple more hours. How did she sell out of cupcakes already?"

Lily wiped her hands on a nearby rag. "From what she said, it started with a face painter who came in for a cup of coffee and decided to try one of the cupcakes. The next thing Mabel knew, the other face painter came in for coffee and a cupcake, followed by the two balloon guys, and then the caricature artists. Each one came with a tale of how the other guy raved about the cupcakes. Looks like we made the right call on the lemon lavender."

"I just wish I wasn't so nervous about all of this." Cindy swiped a lemon lavender doughnut hole from a nearby plate. The first time she'd ever heard of putting lavender in a cake mix, she thought her sister had lost her mind. Once again, her sister proved smarter than the average bear. Everything lemon lavender was a huge hit.

"Any idea how the brunch is going?" Lily asked.

"Oh, yeah. I'm getting a blow-by-blow description from Lucy. Apparently one of the five had to cancel at the last minute but they sent their check anyway. The others are happily eating and chatting up a storm with Alan. From what I understand, the plan is for everyone to ride back to town to gather, then the four donors will receive VIP treatment at the bookstore also. They'll be the first to get their books signed, will have free snacks and sweets, and all the champagne they want to drink. Lucy and Edna have it all worked out. They will definitely be treated like royalty for the rest of the day."

Lily untied her apron and came around by her sister. "I'm not surprised. Edna is so good about making sure everybody who sets foot into her bookstore wants to come back, and Lucy is no slouch when it comes to hospitality."

"What Edna is, is a sweetheart. I'm glad that the big box and online stores haven't driven her out of business." Cindy picked up her pies and headed for the door. "Well, I'd better get moving. I want to check up on the food trucks and street vendors before the crowds really start flowing."

"Which reminds me. Is it true the petting zoo has a baby camel?" Lily held the door for her.

"Yeah. They brought the typical goats, and bunnies, and pigs, but they've also got a camel, an emu, and an alpaca."

"That's like a llama, right?"

Cindy nodded. "Yep. There's a monkey too. I think he might be the biggest hit. I mean, who doesn't love a monkey?"

Shaking her head, Lily chuckled. "The tourists will love all of it."

"From your mouth to God's ears. May they love the fair and happily part with their money." With her hands full, Cindy did her best to wave goodbye to her sister.

Already she could see the bustle of additional activity. Her sources were not exaggerating. The length of downtown Main Street would be closed off to automobile traffic in about an hour, and yet she could already see the extra people mulling about. Cindy paused in front of Floyd's to watch the caricature artist set up by the barber pole. They had an artist at each end of the street. This one was already sketching a cute little girl with pigtails. Considering the hard time the child was having sitting still, the artist was doing a fantastic job. Of course, the mother beamed. Several other folks were pretty impressed too as the line was growing.

Her next stop was Betty's.

The owner of the Cut and Curl came rushing out when she saw her. "I can't believe how many people are coming in for a cut at Fair

Day Pricing. I'm so glad your sister had extra pie. It never occurred to me that my morning clients would all want to buy slices before I even tried to sell them to the tourists."

A handful of shop owners had agreed to sell Lily's baked goods for those who didn't want to walk all the way to the lower end of Main Street. Sort of the town's version of impulse buying.

"This is so exciting. If so far is any sign, we're going to be packed today!" Betty spun on her heel and ran back inside.

Cindy smiled. Packed was definitely the plan. Wanting to check out the petting zoo, she stopped by the balloon guy. Fascinated with how he blew, stretched, twisted, and tied the balloons into fun animals, she was caught by surprise when he twisted a few into a crown and placed it on her head. "Thank you," she muttered, hoping she wasn't blushing.

"Now don't you look pretty as a picture." Louise Franklin came trotting out of the pharmacy to take a picture of Cindy. "This gives me a wonderful idea! If we do this again next year, we're going to have to crown a street festival Queen."

Cindy lightly tapped her makeshift headpiece. Most likely whatever Louise had in mind involved rhinestones and sparkles and something considerably more lavish than her fun crown, but she didn't care. She absolutely loved hers.

"Look," an enthusiastic voice sounded nearby. "Isn't that just adorable?"

The petting zoo, which included exotic animals and education on rescue, rehabilitation, and preservation as well, was only a few feet ahead. It didn't take long to notice what everybody found so adorable. Standing in front of one of the wooden posts supporting the small animal pen was a little boy. The kid had curly blonde locks, a bright orange T-shirt, denim shorts, pudgy little legs, and was swaying left, straightening, then leaning to the right and then back. What everybody was finding so amusing was the monkey on the other side of the post. When the little boy swayed left the monkey tracked his movements. If the boy hid in front of the post, the monkey hid behind it and then if the boy leaned the other way, so did the monkey.

"They're playing peek-a-boo," the same woman's voice said.

Another chimed in with, "I think you're right."

Cindy agreed. Too cute for words, the little boy and the monkey were drawing a crowd. Things were definitely off to a fantastic start. Taking a quick scan around the small animal pen, she noticed a group of young goats. One little girl with a hand-held brush toddled after them in an effort to brush them. An adult handler held a goat in his arms and demonstrated brushing for the children to imitate. The handler had a good grip on the situation. The children, on the other hand, were doing a better job of scattering the goats then luring them in. The baby goat in the young woman's arms blinked. The calming strokes had the goat losing his battle with sleep.

Adorable scenes were scattered everywhere. She sure hoped Alan had some time to see all of this before he needed to report to the bookstore. There wasn't a doubt in her mind that he would love all of this silly behavior by the cute little animals. Besides, in the last week she'd grown to enjoy Alan's company even more than she had the week before, and found herself missing having him here to share the fun. Oh, how she wished he could be here now to squeeze her hand and reassure her all was as good as it looked.

• • • •

Despite all the conversations and impromptu planning sessions that had sprung up this past week, especially at the evening card games at Hart House, Alan had not been truly prepared for his first view of Main Street in its latest rendering. "Wow."

"Isn't it wonderful?" Holding hands with Grant, Violet walked beside Alan. "I knew this would be great. This type of thing is exactly what our sleepy little town needed to put it on the tourism map."

"I think the Pastry Stop has been doing a good job of that." Heather, the cardiologist cousin, had arrived in town just as the brunch was breaking up.

"Agreed." Callie, the high school teacher and coach, had met them in front of the diner with a couple of her students in tow. "But still, this does a lot more for spreading the word far and wide."

Heather stopped and pointed across the street. "Sorry, but I have to run. I promised the mayor I'd check in at the first aid station. That will take me all of five minutes, then I'm meeting Jake at the hardware store. We'll catch up with the rest of you a little later."

"Sounds like a plan." Callie nodded. "Has anyone heard from Cindy?"

"She texted me a few minutes ago that we have to check out the petting zoo." Violet lifted her phone into the air. "Apparently the baby camel and alpaca are too adorable."

As appealing as a menagerie of young animals might be, what Alan really cared about was seeing Cindy before he had to report to the bookstore. Last night he'd had a long visit with Edna the owner. They'd agreed that if they ran out of books, he would remain for as long as the store was open and autograph a paper signature plate for the fan to place inside a book at another time. Though he didn't mind spending hours in the quaint shop, he very much wanted to see Cindy first. He almost felt like a junky needing a fix before he had to dive into dealing with the real world.

"There she is." Violet pointed at Cindy not far away from them.

A few shops ahead, in what was usually a parking lot, Cindy stood with a couple and two kids, waving in front of the petting zoo. His heart did the usual two-step it always did at the sight of her. And to think, only a couple of weeks ago he was ready to give up on fresh air and his muse and head home. Alone. Waving back, he stopped himself from quickening his pace. She may not care for him as much as he cared for her, but he was positive she liked him, hopefully *really* liked him. Still, no sense making a fool of himself in front of the whole town by running down the street like a character in a greeting card commercial.

Surrounded by friends and her family, he didn't dare do anything more than reach for her hand as her family huddled around her. "You look great," he whispered. "It all does."

"Thanks." She squeezed his fingers and smiled. "I needed to hear that."

"This is my cousin Iris, her fiancé Eric, and Gavin and Emily. They've been on vacation in Florida."

The blonde woman sucked in her lips at the introduction and he wasn't sure if she was the only bashful female in the family or if she knew something her cousin didn't. "Alan Peterson. Nice to meet you."

"Seems you've caused quite a commotion around here," Iris said, a confident smile taking over her face.

So she wasn't bashful. "Sorry about that."

"Nonsense," Cindy added. "Commotion is exactly what we need this weekend."

"Aren't these guys the cutest?" Violet took Emily's hand in hers, and ushered the group closer to the attendant.

If Alan remembered what he'd been told about Iris and her new mate, it was the children's uncle who handed the young woman a few dollars in exchange for food to feed the baby goats roaming at their feet.

Violet and Iris promptly lowered themselves to the animal's level, helping the children hold out the kibble.

Alan had to admit, the animals were cute. The whole point of the fair was to raise money, and buying food from the petting zoo was a part of that. He gave the attendant a bill and waved for her to keep the change.

"Be careful," Cindy warned. "If you give an inch they'll—"

"Hey," Violet squeaked, falling back on her rear as one of the goats absconded with the whole bag.

"Take a mile," Cindy finished her sentence through muffled laughter.

Still sitting on the ground, Violet's rigid expression gave way to fits of laughter as the goats polished off the brown paper bag and began battling over the food in Iris's hand.

Both children's eyes rounded like cartoon characters at Violet sprawled on the ground before sputtering with laughter and promptly falling down with Violet.

"I'm not sure I'm willing to get in on this," Alan chuckled, keeping the food-filled paper bag high above the ground.

"Let me." Cindy reached into the bag and pulling out a handful of pellets, smiled at him before turning to the animals who would have gladly eaten the offering, bag and all. Sniffing out their next meal, the four legged garbage disposals abandoned Violet and the children and hurried toward Cindy.

Alan had an absurd urge to pull her out of the way of the harmless, but perpetually hungry, kids. Leaning over to join the fun, from the corner of his eye he spotted a curly haired little boy gleefully running past them. The nearest adult, a lone woman stood by the pen with the camel, carrying a little girl on her hip. Alan had the distinct feeling that she had no idea her son was making a beeline for the goat pen.

"Uh oh." Cindy's eyes widened.

It took Alan a second too long to put two and two together. Cindy snapped to her full height and spun about toward the gate, giving chase to the little boy. Another second and they would have cut him off at the proverbial pass. As it was, the blond haired munchkin maneuvered the latch with the same ease he probably would have used to open adult-proof medication bottles.

"Oh, no." Already on the ground, Violet flung herself forward in an effort to grab the nearest little goat that slid through her grip like a greased owl.

Hands in the air, the two children on either side of her giggled with delight at Violet's latest predicament at the same time the gleeful culprit tore off after the first escapee, leaving the gate wide open.

"Quick," Callie hollered to Violet's fiancé. "Grab one!"

A gray and white streak zoomed past the startled man, sending him slipping on the muddied straw beneath his feet.

"Grant!" Violet tripped over one of the slower goats running toward the open gate, and balancing herself, scooped the little guy up into her arms and came to a skidding halt in front of her fiancé. "Are you okay?"

"Fine." Grant spotted the open gate, the baby goats bolting toward freedom, and lunging forward, pounced on the only kid within reach.

"I got one!" Across the way, Callie cradled a baby goat in her arms.

Iris and Eric each held on to one of the children.

"Shut the gate!" a voice hollered just in time to stop the remaining goat from following one ecstatic toddler already scurrying down Main Street with Cindy in hot pursuit and Alan on her heels.

"Billy!" the little boy's mother finally noticed her wayward son.

Like the Red Sea in biblical times, the people mulling about parted as the goat and little boy pushed their way down Main Street. The child's giggles grew louder and the goat followed him as though they'd been best buddies all of their short lives. Finally, Cindy's long legs matched the little boy's head start, and she scooped him up.

Alan came up on them, and grabbing the escaped goat, joined Cindy and the little boy, giggling and laughing all the way back to the small animals' pen. Except for the squirming goat, the picture they painted—him, Cindy and the little boy—was more than appealing. He liked it. A lot.

"Billy." At the zoo entrance, the mother lifted her son into the double-seater stroller and turned to Cindy. "Thank you."

"Yes." The attendant reached for the goat. "Thank you. I'm the only one here. The others are grabbing a quick lunch before the crowds arrive."

"Glad we could help," Cindy offered quickly.

The attendant double checked the latch and set the baby goat down by the others.

"Well, that was different." Violet brushed some dirt from her slacks then threaded her hand with Grant's. "I think that's a first for me."

"You and me both." Grant smiled.

Callie came up beside them, wiping her hands on a paper towel. "We should do this again some time," she teased.

Smiling, Iris shook her head. "I have to admit. It was rather entertaining to watch."

"And this," the uncle got down on his haunches, "is why you guys need to always stay close to one of us in public places."

Both kids nodded at their father, but Alan had a feeling given the chance, any red-blooded child would rather chase goats.

"I suppose we should be thankful it wasn't the exotic animals," Cindy said.

"She has a point," Alan agreed. "Even baby camels run pretty quickly."

"Oh," Violet cooed, now across the way, petting the much larger animal, "and it's so soft. The alpaca too."

"Be careful, though." Callie waved her finger in the direction of the two animals. "They spit."

"Oh, no." Cindy's eyes opened wide.

Everyone turned in the direction of Cindy's gaze. The same little boy had climbed out of the stroller, made his way to the pen with the larger petting animals, and with the dexterity of a safecracker, swung the gate open.

"And here we go again," multiple voices mumbled.

CHAPTER SEVENTEEN

T his was not what Cindy had signed up for when this fundraising idea had come together. Mouth hanging open, all the color drained from the attendant's face before it snapped shut and she hurriedly closed the gate. Panic in her eyes, she looked from the penned animals still in place to the street ahead. Only three animals had slipped by before the gate had been secured once again, but the gal could do simple math; there was only one of her and a bunch of other animals in need of supervising.

"We've got this," Cindy yelled to her.

Relief washing over her face, she nodded then turned and stormed toward the clueless mom.

Quickly surveying the situation, Cindy pointed down the road. "Looks like Cole and his buddy are already chasing the emu."

"Good," Violet huffed, already rushing toward the street, her fiancé at her side. "Those suckers are really fast. Grant and I will go after the alpaca."

"Sounds good," Cindy shouted at her cousin, then prepared to bolt after the camel running in the opposite direction. She looked up at Alan. "Want to catch a camel?"

Grinning like a little kid offered the keys to the candy store, he nodded, grabbed her hand and leading the way, darted down Main Street. "Camels can get a good trot going. Funny looking, but fast. We'd better hurry."

"Maybe this time someone will stop him rather than just step aside." She couldn't believe how many strangers earlier on Main had been willing to let a little boy run by them without stopping to see if something was wrong.

"You can't really blame them." Alan smiled, his gaze steady on the camel ahead. "These people are not locals. Since we were already giving chase, they probably thought *we* were the parents."

She hadn't considered that. At all. Though she would admit, just a little while ago, as they'd made their way back to the parking lot where the zoo was set up, she'd liked the feel of Alan and her with a child and a pet. Though in her world she would have preferred a Golden Retriever like Lady and Sarge. Or maybe something hypo-allergenic like a Golden Doodle.

"Oh, no." Alan pointed. The animal hung a left and galloped through the open double doors of the shop ahead.

Cindy held her breath and picked up her speed. Of all the shops the animal could have gone into, it chose to go through that one. The Crystal Emporium.

A loud, startled screech sounded from inside the gift shop. From experience, Cindy knew the place was loaded with fine china, crystals, figurines and enough breakables to leave the fundraiser seriously in the financial hole.

"This can't be good," Alan muttered at her side.

Turning on her heel, she flew into the shop and skidded to a stop. *What the…*

Alan looked left, then right, then settled his gaze on her. "This is the right shop?"

Surely if an animal as large as a camel, even a baby camel, came prancing through a china shop, there would be plenty of collateral damage. Except, not here. Every glass shelf, figurine and point of sale display was intact as it should be. The only reason Cindy was convinced she hadn't been mistaken about which store the camel had entered was the wide-eyed shock on the clerk's face and the shaky finger pointing to a rear doorway.

"Come on." Alan waved at her and sprinted forward.

Stepping over the threshold of the back door into the alley, Cindy stopped short behind Alan.

Hand extended in front of him, he cooed, "Hey, fellow," slowly moving forward. The camel had stopped at a trash can and lifting his head, eyed Alan with a mixture of curiosity and suspicion.

Something told Cindy this little guy might give his trainers a run for their money more often than not. "Remember, they spit," she said softly.

Alan turned to look over his shoulder at her. "That may be the least of my troubles." He pointed to the ground nearby.

Though she didn't know enough about camels to figure out how he'd done it, apparently fishing through the trash cans, the camel managed to squirm his way out of the harness and the easiest way to control him. If they could get close enough. Slowly, Alan inched forward, talking softly to the animal now watching him with more interest than the scraps in the garbage.

"Atta, boy." Alan kept his gaze level with the curious animal as he leaned forward and picked up the end of the rope, then cautiously inched forward another step.

The camel took a step back and Cindy was pretty sure the game was now on. This guy had no interest in being haltered again. "Be careful."

Before she could give any further instructions, the camel's lips parted and spit flew the short distance at an unprepared Alan.

Wiping his face, he took a second before laughing. "I see what you mean."

"They kick too." She smiled.

He rolled his eyes skyward. "Marvy."

Still smiling, she shrugged. "Want me to try?"

"Nope." Alan smiled at the camel while speaking to her. "The gauntlet, so to speak, has been thrown."

Cindy pressed her lips between her teeth to stifle a laugh.

"Come on, fella." Alan barely moved, hiding the rope behind his back. "I bet you like your ears scratched, don't you?"

She wasn't all too sure of that one, but couldn't wait to see how it turned out. He was talking to the camel the same way he spoke to Frick and Frack.

Taking another slow half step, Alan got close enough for his fingers to gently touch the camel's neck. "See. That's not so bad, is it?"

His fingers dug into the soft fur another minute before the animal spit and pulled away.

"Didn't your mother teach you it's not polite to spit?" He pulled a handkerchief from his pocket and cleaned his face.

Cindy didn't know very many men who still carried handkerchiefs. She liked that he was a throwback to a different time. Maybe adapting to small town life might not be such a challenge for him after all.

"Shall we try that again?" Alan braved facing the spitting camel once again. This time sliding his hand along the long furry neck. "We can do this."

The camel's leg moved and before she could shout a warning, Alan shifted out of the way of a half-hearted kick.

"That wasn't very nice," he softly chastised the uncooperative creature.

"Maybe if you can get him to sit?"

For the first time since he got within reach of the animal, Alan turned his eyes toward her. "You're kidding?"

"No." She shook her head. "I've read that sometimes it's easier to harness a difficult camel if he's on the ground."

"You've read up on harnessing camels?" The curious lift of his brows almost made her laugh.

"I read a lot." She shrugged.

He returned his attention to the dromedary who seemed more interested in Alan and her interaction than escaping again. Alan gave his neck a gentle pat. "You heard the lady. Sit."

To her great surprise, the camel did as commanded.

"Well, I'll be." Alan scratched the camel's neck in earnest. "Aren't you a good boy." A few more seconds of cooperative camel and Alan had the harness around his head. "We did it."

"Not *we*. You." She closed the gap between them and threw her arms around him. "My hero!"

The camel pushed to its wobbly feet and stared at them.

"Yeah, well." Still hanging onto the rope, he slid one arm around her. "I don't know about the hero thing."

About to convince him otherwise, she noticed the camel's lips perch at the same moment Alan did. In a single movement that caught her off guard, Alan swerved her around, taking a direct hit while blocking her from the onslaught of camel spit.

"See?" She smiled at him. "My hero."

"Or just a delusional author crazy enough to chase after a camel."

"That too." She grinned.

Maybe he was just a little bit crazy, but this kind of crazy she could use in her life.

• • • •

"My goodness," Edna shook her head, "I haven't had this much foot traffic in a day since Nora Roberts came through a decade ago!"

Even if Alan wasn't a romance writer, he'd be an idiot not to recognize the compliment. Whether a person was a fan of Nora or her alter ego JD Robb didn't matter, the woman was an icon in the publishing world. "Thank you, but I think credit is more likely because people love a good cause."

"And a good book," she countered.

"Thank you. I had fun." He'd actually had way more fun than he'd expected. While sitting in a chair signing his name for hours wasn't the most comfortable of experiences, after the early exclusive signing for the larger donors, Edna had kept him supplied with everything from pink lemonade and sweet tea to some of the most delectable cookies and muffins, no doubt from Lily's bakery. He'd probably put on five pounds but enjoyed every bite. Even with the delicious treats, the most entertaining had been the visits from the town folks he'd gotten to know during his stay. Floyd the barber had become as popular as his TV reference. So much so that many of the customers requested he sign their books as well. And though Alan had heard Ralph telling stories over cards at the lake of his days on the commuter trains back in the day, none had been quite as entertaining as when he played to a larger audience. A time or two Alan had been so engrossed in the stories that he'd forget why he was here and had stopped signing to just listen. Fortunately, whoever had been at his side had been equally enraptured by the storytelling.

Standing in the corner, quietly watching his conversation with Edna, Cindy leaned against a wall of books and smiled at him. Not since he was a goofy teen had a mere glance at a pretty girl sent his heart racing while at the same time fearing if he moved he'd trip over his own feet.

"I'd better run." Edna took a step back. "I have a few things to attend to. Don 't want to miss the final drum roll."

Alan watched the woman scurry away before meeting Cindy

halfway across the store.

"I heard you were a big hit."

"I don't know about that," he answered.

"I do. Edna already sent in her numbers for the first part of the day. I suspect she's working up the final donation numbers now."

All afternoon folks had enthusiastically been sharing updates on the large campaign thermometer in front of the old city hall building. "Last I heard, the fundraiser was doing really well."

Cindy sucked in a long slow breath. "I'm almost afraid to look but with all the high fives, thumbs up, whistles and smiles I've been getting, it should be pretty good."

"I think it's going to be better than good."

"I sure hope so." Cindy smiled slowly. "Hungry?"

He couldn't stop the laugh that erupted. "Hardly. I've been fed all afternoon long."

Cindy giggled. "I bet."

"How about you? Want some company for dinner?"

"I actually have snacked my way through the food trucks most of the day." She smiled sheepishly. "Those zeppoles are irresistible."

His brows buckled.

"Every region has a different version," she quickly explained. "Funnel cake, beignets, zeppoles. All are basically fried dough with their own twist, and lots of sugar on top."

"I have to admit, I have a weakness for beignets. Perhaps I should sample one of your zeppoles. You know, for scientific purposes."

A huge grin took over her face. "Sounds like a good idea. For science, of course."

Taking her hand in his, they strolled out the door and down the street, weaving through the crowds. The town was packed. Folks had come to spend money, support a good cause, and have a good time. Every age from strollers to walkers was represented, and all had bright smiles. His girl had done good. *His girl.* He really liked the sound of that. He'd liked an awful lot about not just today, but every day since she'd rescued him from an oversized feline.

By the time they reached the square in front of city hall, they'd been greeted and congratulated by half the town, found the room to nibble on more tasty treats, and he was just about to buy her a paper rose when he heard her gasp. "What is it?" He spun around.

Jaw hanging slightly open, her hand over her mouth, Cindy's other arm pointed straight ahead.

Following the direction of her dangling finger, he spotted the reason for her reaction. The thermometer was a good three quarters colored in. "Guess that's more than you expected."

Silently, she nodded, her hand still covering her mouth.

"There's more."

She turned to look at him, snapping her mouth shut before forming words. "More?"

The sound of someone tapping on a microphone reverberated through the speakers that had been set up to play easy listening music or the live performances on the makeshift stages.

"Ladies and Gentlemen." The mayor stood at the tiny stage, grinning out at the crowd slowly gathering around her. "As you can see from our little thermometer, today has been a glorious day for the Lawford Mountain Wildlife Center for Rescue, Rehabilitation and Preservation."

Stepping up onto the stage, Mr. Perfect came into view.

"What's he still doing here?" Somehow Alan didn't believe for a minute the guy cared one iota about the small town of Lawford.

"He's been a big help all afternoon. Filling in where ever needed. Helping me transport things back and forth."

"Transport," he mumbled.

"For someone dripping with money, he's a nice guy."

"Hm," he grunted. *Nice guy.* When the man's gaze landed on Cindy and his smile widened, Alan knew exactly why the guy was still here.

Hands shadowing her eyes, the mayor scanned the audience. "Where is Mr. Peterson?"

Catching her eye, he shook his head no.

"Now, don't be bashful," the woman coaxed.

He blew out a sigh and shook his head again.

"I think he needs a little encouragement." She put her hands together and began clapping. Slowly the crowd joined in.

"I don't know what this is about," Cindy whispered, "but you might as well give in."

"You're probably right." Squeezing her hand, he tugged at her arm. "I'm not doing this alone."

Cindy's eyes widened but she followed along. Just one of the things he'd come to love about her. Unwavering support and trust came naturally for her, and when it was cast in his direction he felt ten feet tall.

"In the meantime," the mayor continued, "we've been honored by a very generous donor today."

Mr. Perfect stepped forward and handed a piece of paper to the mayor. The way the woman's eyes rounded and her brows shot up high enough to kiss her hairline, it had to be a whopper of a donation.

"Oh, my." The town leader waved the paper as if the people in the crowd could see the tiny print. "We have a pledge for twenty thousand dollars."

Perfect cleared his throat.

"Though there is one condition," the bubbling woman smiled.

At the top of the stairs, Alan stepped aside for Cindy to stand beside him and resisted the urge to block her from Perfect's view.

"A dinner date with our good Dr. Nelson." The way the mayor grinned at Cindy, anyone would think that was a great idea.

It wasn't, but Alan had to bite his tongue. It wasn't his dream, and Cindy wasn't his woman.

"I, uh," Cindy held her hand to her chest, but didn't let go of Alan's hand, "don't know what to say."

He supposed *no* would be asking too much. After all, the only thing on the table was dinner. Even if Perfect wanted to delude himself, of that much Alan was sure. He'd just bought a very expensive dinner—and only dinner—companion.

Cindy smiled, but didn't say another word.

"Well," the mayor continued, "we should probably move on to our other big announcement."

Faces in the crowd stared, eyes filled with curiosity and confusion.

"Our own Mr. Peterson." She waved him to come closer. "You don't mind me calling you that, do you? After all, we feel as though you're one of us now."

He smiled at the woman and planted himself at the opposite end from Perfect, keeping Cindy at his other side. "Not at all. I too feel as though I belong."

"Isn't that wonderful. And now the news." She waved another sheet of paper she'd been holding. "Our Mr. Peterson, or Peters as many of you know him, was very gracious in donating his time and talents, and now he has made another very generous donation."

Cindy tipped her head, her gaze meeting his.

"Why don't you tell us?" The smiling woman handed him the mic.

"Yes. Of course." He took the microphone and squeezed Cindy's hand. "While I've been here in your lovely town, the lush countryside has been very inspiring. A new idea came to me for a softer, cozier mystery, set right here in Lawford."

The choral gasp of pleasure and surprise from those standing around surprised him.

"It only seemed right that I should repay this wonderful town for the idea. I've pledged my royalties for the first book, and a portion for the remainder of the series to the wildlife center."

Cindy's jaw dropped and her eyes twinkled with unshed tears. "Really?"

"Really." He nodded.

From a narrow table behind her, the mayor lifted a glass sculpture around six inches high and handed one to him and another to Mr. Perfect. "From a grateful community for your generosity, please accept these little tokens. Our own glass craftsman from the Crystal Emporium, Max Porter, has made these especially for you in remembrance of the first annual Lawford Street Fair."

Both Alan and Mr. Perfect muttered a polite thank you.

"On that note," the mayor announced to the crowd, "let's get on with the fun." The mayor shuffled behind them, ushering everyone off the stage.

"I should put this someplace safe." He laid a hand across the small of Cindy's back and steered her toward the lot where his car was parked. Mr. Perfect closed in on their heels.

"Is that as generous as I think?" she said softly, so the other generous donor wouldn't hear.

He laughed. "Probably. I figure there are going to be an awful lot of expenses once the place is built. Staff, supplies. You'll need money."

"Thank you."

"There is one condition," he said quietly.

"Dinner?" she teased.

From the corner of his eyes he could see Perfect wince. "I was thinking more of your approval."

Tilting her face to steal a glance as they walked, her brows buckled and her gaze intensified.

He stopped close to his car, twirling her around to face him. "I'd like to stay in Lawford."

"You would?" Her face softened and her eyes twinkled. "I'd like that."

"Then I guess the money is yours."

"That's it?"

He shook his head. "There's more, but it has nothing to do with the donation and will have to wait until we don't have a crowd of people milling about." He popped the trunk open with the key fob. "Then, after you've grown to find me as irresistible as I find you, I'll have a more serious question for you."

This time her eyes popped open wide and she melted into his side. "I like the sound of that."

"Looks to me, like I have my answer." Mr. Perfect paused beside them, and to Alan's surprise flashed a sincere smile. "Can't blame a guy for trying."

"I can't say that I do," he answered.

Mr. Perfect turned and froze. His gaze landed on the trunk. Eyes widening, his mouth fell open and then his head shot up to Alan and Cindy. Slowly, a sly grin replaced the stunned expression. "Aren't you two the sly ones?" Without another word, Perfect turned toward the limousine parked up the street.

Looking at Harvey tossed in the trunk, his hands and feet tied, Cindy and Alan burst out laughing.

"Oh brother." Cindy leaned into him. "Who knows what he must be thinking."

Alan whispered against her temple, "That I love you, Hyacinth

Nelson."

Tipping her head up, her gaze lingered on his. "I like the sound of that too."

CHAPTER EIGHTEEN ~ EPILOGUE

Sunny blue skies shined down on the Point. The General wouldn't have stood for anything else on a wedding day for his granddaughters. He was now batting two for two.

"It's going to be a beautiful day." Grams took her seat opposite her husband at the other end of the table.

"Any day is beautiful for a wedding." Lucy set some serving utensils on the table and flashed a toothy grin at the two engaged women at the table, neither of which had announced their wedding plans.

At least Iris and the love of her life were spared Lucy's attention. Unlike today's massive summer wedding, Iris and Eric had opted for a very short engagement and tied the knot on the Point a couple of weeks ago with only a few close friends and family in attendance. The day had reminded Rose of a garden party. Small, fun, and terribly romantic.

When Iris and Eric had initially announced their plans, for the first time in her life Rose had seen her grandmother on the verge of apoplexy. Once the two had explained that making their family official wasn't something they wanted to wait for in order to put a big shindig together, Grams had acquiesced and given her blessing to the small church wedding and sweet celebration that followed.

"All right." The General raised his wine glass. "To my girls. Each and every one of you has brought nothing but joy to my life."

"I don't remember him saying that when he caught us skinny dipping back in high school," Cindy mumbled to Alan at her side.

His hand drawing gentle circles across her palm, Rose wasn't sure he'd even heard what she'd said. Ignoring that if the two sat any closer they'd be in each other's laps, Rose leaned in and whispered to her cousin. "Shh. Old Eagle Eyes has bionic ears too."

Without skipping a beat, the General held his smile, but managed to cast an I-heard-that glance in her direction. Their grandfather had insisted on a traditional family meal before this evening's wedding. Despite all the preparations under way, and the enormous task of getting eight bridesmaids and one bride ready for a sunset wedding, it hadn't occurred to anyone to protest. Somehow starting out Lily's big day surrounded in good food and loving family made perfect sense.

"Cole," the General shifted his attention to his very soon to be grandson-in-law, "I am proud to have you as my grandson. Welcome."

Another thing that seemed perfectly right. There were no in-laws in this family. For the General and Grams, Cole was already a Hart.

"I'm still not sure how it could have been only yesterday that you wore out your Easy Bake Oven making pretend wedding cakes for your sisters, but," Aunt Virginia blinked back a tear, "I am delighted that the rest of your life at Cole's side will be everything you dreamed of. I love you, baby girl."

Lily blinked, pinched her lips, swallowed, and mouthed, "I love you too."

At that moment, Cole turned to his bride-to-be and stared down at her with such intensity that Rose wondered if two people had ever been more in love. Of course, that single and absurd thought flew by the wayside as soon as she caught a glimpse of her sisters. Heather and Violet. Both locked gazes with their fiancés, and as the old saying went, a picture was worth a thousand words. Rose was pretty sure if the room caught on fire, not one of the two couples would have noticed.

The clatter of dishes and plates handed about echoed in the room. Not terribly hungry and a tad on edge with all that still needed to be taken care of, Rose took a sip of wine and glanced at the cousins she loved like sisters. Cindy was the one with the glow of a brand spanking new ring on her finger. Who was Rose kidding? They all had it. If she was sure of nothing else, she was convinced her cousins were well on their way to a lifetime marriage like their parents and grandparents.

"Earth to Rose." Poppy held a dish of Lucy's potato salad in front of her.

"Sorry." She grabbed the dish, dumped a small scoop on her plate and having gone full circle round the table, set it on one of the quilted squares. Bless her grandmother, but she'd been bound and determined to quilt the old fashioned way by hand. Except, halfway through her first project Grams decided her fingertips didn't have enough blood to survive. They now had a hefty supply of quilted trivets.

"That's an awfully serious expression." Cindy let go of Alan's hand and leaned forward. "Do we need to take care of something?" Like Heather, Cindy was one of the serious ones in the family. It shouldn't have surprised her that her cousin was ready to get down to business.

"Nope, just contemplating the immortality of the crab."

Her grandmother grinned at her. The girls had always loved that expression as children. It took Rose a good long time, too long, to realize that wasn't at all what her grandmother often contemplated.

"Well no time for lollygagging." Lucy now carried a large platter of pulled pork. "The photographer is on his way and the rental place people are here setting up chairs."

"Yes, ma'am." The General saluted and most of the people around the table laughed. Today wouldn't be the first time Lucy had been the one truly giving the orders.

"About time." Rose pushed to her feet. "I just need a minute to give them a few instructions."

"That's not your job today." Lily gestured for Rose to sit. "If I can let someone else do the baking, you can let someone else do the designating."

"Easier said than done." She sat.

"Tell me about it," Zinnia mumbled. This was only the second or third time she'd been to the lake in months. Rose was going to have to pull her aside later and find out what exactly was going on.

"Don't you worry." The General leaned left and scratched Lady's head. "You'll get your chance with the fishing auction. Then you can run things any way you want."

"I still don't understand how you talked me into that. I know art, not fish."

Cindy chuckled beside her. "Shh or you might be spending the rest of this weekend learning about fish."

Her cousin had a point. That was one thing she'd avoided

growing up and was more than happy to continue to do so.

By the time lunch was over, the family descended on the kitchen like an army of ants. Next stop was the adjoining bedrooms that had been separated for the bridal party.

"I forgot my mascara." Cindy fished through a makeup bag.

Poppy shot her arm out at her sister. "Use mine."

"Thanks."

"Will you be careful." Iris smacked at her sister Violet holding the curling iron. "That thing is hot."

"It's supposed to be," Violet shot back.

Zinnia hefted the straps of the lavender dress over her shoulders. "I need someone to zip me up."

"I will." Callie brushed the wrinkles away from her own dress and turned to her cousin.

It had only taken a few hours of primping and laughing to get everyone ready. Since it was impossible to pick a favorite among the eight granddaughters, there was no maid of honor for this event. Each engaged or married member of the bridal party was to meet their significant other at the bottom of the stairs and proceed to the Point. Cole's firemen buddies were partnered up with the single bridesmaids.

"You look stunning." Rose helped Lily straighten the edges of the veil.

"Thank you."

"I hear music," Cindy announced. "Places everyone."

Rose fell in behind Cindy and slowly they made their way to the end of the hall. At the bottom of the stairs, the men were lined up, looking much more relaxed than Rose felt. Maybe they were just better at hiding their excitement than she was. Only a few steps behind her cousin, she couldn't help but see how Alan's eyes lit when Cindy came off the bottom step.

"You are amazing," Alan whispered, extending his arm.

The three single words spoken with such tenderness, coupled with the fire in his gaze, gave Rose goose bumps. *Some day.*

Extending his arm as Alan had for her cousin, Payton Taylor smiled at her sans the look of adoration in his eyes. "Ready?"

"Yes," she smiled at him. "I think I am."

From Lily's Recipe Box

APFEL KUCHEN
(German Apple Cake)

What you'll need:

2cups flour
½ teaspoon salt (Only for unsalted butter)
3 teaspoons baking powder
¾ cup + 2 tablespoons sugar
8 tablespoons butter – softened (see note below)
2/3 cup whole milk
1 egg
4-5 large granny smith apples: peeled, cored and sliced
1 teaspoon cinnamon

Instructions:

Combine unsifted flour, baking powder, salt, 2 tablespoons sugar, and mix until blended.
Cut in 6 tablespoons softened butter (not melted).
Mix until it resembles coarse breadcrumbs.
Combine egg and milk in separate bowl. Stir.
Pour egg mixture into flour mixture until blended. It will be very sticky.
Spread into greased 8x12x2 inch pan.
Arrange apples in rows overlapping slightly and press into dough.
Spread 2 tablespoons melted butter evenly over apples.
Mix ¾ cup sugar with cinnamon until totally blended. Pour over apples.

Bake at 400 degrees for 30 minutes.

Lily's note: If you use unsalted butter, add ½ teaspoon of salt. If you use salted butter, do not add salt.

Excerpt from ROSE

"\"Watch your step." The voice attached to the tool-clad man in a yellow hard hat carried loudly across the small workspace. The man hadn't even bothered to look up, but staring at Rose Preston's feet, he shook his head. Only a construction worker could view a two-inch wedge heel with the same disdain as that of a five-inch stiletto.

"Thanks," she responded calmly. What she actually wanted to say was *I'll match my careful steps in heels to your steel-toed stomps any day*. Walking through a construction site had nothing on running through the woods at night in flip flops with only the moon to guide her path. For a fraction of a minute she allowed herself the luxury of letting her mind drift back to the youthful days of lakeside summers. The next moment, she glanced at her wrist and sighed. If all went well she'd be on her way to Hart Land in little more than an hour.

Not truly a vacation, but even working at the lake was a joy. The distasteful image of a string of fresh-caught fish flashed in her mind. *At least she hoped so.* Tablet in hand and satisfied with the small exhibit's progress, she proceeded directly to the conference room.

Halfway down the main hall, Sarah, the best right-hand-man a woman could ask for, clutched a color-coded binder to her chest and fell into step beside her. "Jim texted that he's caught in the back up from a six car pile up on I-93. I told him not to worry, we got this."

Without breaking pace, Rose cast a sideways glance in Sarah's direction. She'd feel much better about that comment if she wasn't about to spend the next two weeks dealing with… fisherman.

Sarah reached the double doors first and shoved them open, stepping aside for Rose to pass and take a seat at the massive table already buried in stacks of files and photos. "Did you get the condition report?"

"I did. Looks good." She nodded, studying the photos spread out on the table and running the new layout in her mind. They had a lot of work to do and she'd only had one cup of coffee this morning. Stretching her neck from left to right, she spotted the brewing pot of caffeine and headed over. "All the works look to be here."

"Yes. I did a walk through yesterday and confirmed." Sarah ruffled through papers in the binder, slid one out, and placed it on the table. Yes, they both used technology and electronics, but like Rose, Sarah was a tactile person and if heaven forbid the cyber world ever crashed, she and Sarah would still have everything they needed at their fingertips.

Feeling reassured at that silly idea, Rose turned back and set a mug down in front of Sarah, then holding the paper in one hand returned to the coffee station. "This may be the first time customs hasn't found at least one thing to give me indigestion." Turning back, she set the sugar in front of her assistant curator.

"Thanks." Sarah tore the packet open and poured it into her mug. By the time she'd stirred it in, Rose had set the creamer beside her as well.

Next they went over all the photo captions for the exhibit publications. "It will be up to you to follow up with the printers. I'll have some access to internet—"

"I'll stay on top of it." Sarah took a sip of her coffee.

The woman kept pace with Rose and was the only reason the thought of leaving for two weeks before a new, albeit small, exhibit didn't give her apoplexy. From there, they pored over public inquires, moved on to copyrights for the music, then scents for a visceral experience only to have the idea nixed for multiple reasons.

When the phone pinged from the conservator at the loan museum, Sarah took the call and once again the ease with which she handled the conversation gave Rose one less thing to toil over.

A brief interruption ensued over exhibit supports with the designer and by the time lunch rolled around, they'd discussed marketing materials, the media preview, and personally checked the exhibit storage area. Her stomach growled and she knew another cup of java was not what her body needed.

The landline rang and Sarah was first to reach the phone.

"Good morning, sir." Her face brightened. "Yes, sir. Good to hear your voice too."

Rose didn't have to hear anything more to know who was on the other end of the line. Wondering why her grandfather hadn't called her cell, she glanced down at her phone and saw two missed calls. She'd placed it on silent no vibrate in order to get through this morning's agenda quickly. The exhibit designer was marching in her direction carrying two different sized white panels. Sucking in a deep sigh, she mouthed to Sarah 'tell him I'll call back when I'm on the road' and turned to deal with how major an impact would shifting from four foot to six foot display boards affect the original design. Suddenly any amount of time with fish and fisherman was looking really good to her.

• • • •

Straightening, Logan Buchanan stretched his shoulders and rolled his head left then right. It had been ages since he'd ridden a fence line with the crew and even longer since he'd done repairs. Rising before the sun and saddling a horse had been the easy part of this day. Once upon a time, he'd spent more time on horseback than at the keyboard. For as long as he could remember, working beside his dad was as routine for him and his siblings as Saturday morning cartoons for the rest of the world.

"I don't know about you, but I'm ready for a snack." For Cal, snack was cowboy code for could eat a cow.

"Thinking the same." It had been hours since the big breakfast Maggie had made for everyone, and his stomach was beginning to protest.

"Didn't think we'd get that much work done." Cal slipped his gloves off and tucked them into his back pocket. He might be one of the youngest hands on the ranch, but he had the diplomacy of someone older and wiser. He could have just come out and said he'd expected working with a desk jockey like Logan to slow them down.

Logan chuckled. "I guess it's like riding a bike. Some things you don't forget."

"Guess so." The kid checked his phone, slid it into his other pocket and then reached into his saddle bag for a bottle of water, his gaze scanning the distance for signs of lunch.

Logan didn't blame him. They'd put in a hard morning's work and he might easily *snack* on a side of beef himself.

"How you holding up?"

So much for youthful diplomacy. After all, he wasn't *that* old. Except for a little stiffness in muscles that hadn't been used since the last time he'd chipped in to work the cattle or the fences, it felt good to get away from the office and away from his computer. Not that he didn't love all things electronic, but Texas fresh air and working the land was in his blood as much as the telecom corridor. If he had to choose between the two, it would be like asking which leg would he cut off.

The two ranch hands who had worked the fence line on the other side of the north pasture rode up in a four-wheeler. He wasn't sure who was younger, the two hands or his favorite boots. No wonder Cal was treating him like an old man.

"Hank called. He's bringing lunch."

In the distance, the dust kicked up. The ranch suburban came to a stop and Hank, the senior foreman who had been with the ranch since Logan was tall enough to mount his own horse, climbed out and walked over. His gait was that of a man who had spent more time on a horse than behind the wheel of a motor vehicle. "Maggie made her peach cobbler for dessert."

Whistles, hoots, and wide grins broke out. Logan had to admit, the woman made a mean cobbler. The hatch open and the tailgate down, the back of the suburban hosted a buffet spread fit for a king, or a hardworking cowboy.

"I hear you're heading up north?" Hank asked, filling up his own plate.

"Yeah. Gramps and I are going to help out a buddy of his throwing his first fishing tournament."

Hank shook his head. "I can understand an afternoon at the creek, but I want to eat my catch not weigh it."

Funny how he'd felt the same way until he'd done his first tourney with his grandfather.

"Boy, what are you doing?" Hank frowned at Cal.

A biscuit in one hand, chomping away, the kid was playing a game on his phone with his other hand. "Bait and Fish."

Hank's brow rose high on his forehead. "What?"

"It's a game," one of the hands answered. "Everyone's playing it. It's bigger than Angry Birds."

"Angry what?" This time Hank's brows buckled in confusion. Poor guy didn't stand a chance.

Suddenly Logan felt much younger. Though he had to admit, it wasn't often anyone found a cowhand using his lunch break to play games on his phone. At least the kid had good taste.

Hank's head snapped around to Logan. "And what are you grinning at?"

"Me?" He bit back a smile. "Nothing."

"God…" Cal started, frowning down at his phone.

"You'd better not be thinking of taking the lord's name in vain," Hank snapped.

"I can't get past level five. I've been at this forever. Keep falling out of the canoe."

"Let me see what you're doing." Logan leaned to one side for a better view of the kid's screen.

"You play?" Cal asked.

"Some." He shrugged. "Don't go so fast. That's the mistake everyone makes. This isn't speed, it's endurance. And don't waste your bait."

Cal frowned and shoving the last morsel of biscuit in his mouth, used two hands to tackle the game. Five minutes later the kid threw his arms into the air and sprang to his feet. "Level six, here I come!"

"Yeah, well." Hank pushed to his feet. "Level six will have to wait till after you finish working this fence line."

"Yes, sir." Without hesitation, Cal slid the phone into his pocket, placed his hat on his head, and just like that, the kid gave way to a hard working cowboy.

There was something to be said for slowing down. His grandfather was probably right. A little time up north would be really good for him. A few hundred fishermen aside, just him, his gramps, and the fish. What more could a man ask for?

• • • •

Some days the idea of returning to horses for transportation held enormous appeal for Rose. Even if the beautiful animals couldn't travel at sixty miles an hour, a good horse could probably get her across Boston in less time than a fast car stuck in rush hour traffic. Which brought a whole other problem to light. Why did they still call it rush hour when the business commute time had become more like rush four-hours. At times like Fridays and holiday weekends—or like today, when there's an accident—rush half-a-day was more appropriate. It had taken most of what should have been the almost three-hour drive to get to the lake just to get out of the Boston area limits.

Now she'd turned off the main highway and onto the country roads that would take her to Hart Land. Already her blood pressure was dropping and she could feel the tension that had taken residence in her shoulders easing away. So many shades of green hung over the drive; she loved Mother Nature's canopy. This was the way traveling should be. Not even a bumpy ride in a hundred year old carriage would have mucked it up—or the ringing of her cell phone. Hitting accept call on her steering wheel, she smiled at the General's name on her dashboard. "I'm almost there."

"And good afternoon to you too. The least you can do is wait for me to ask the question before answering."

"And why would I want to do that when I already know the question? Cutting to the chase saves time."

"Young lady, this is not Boston. Life on the mountain is not about saving time."

Wasn't that the truth. She sucked in a long deep breath of fresh mountain air. "Yes, sir."

"Now." She could hear his hands clap together enthusiastically.

No doubt he'd used his laptop to call her. Ever since his Annapolis reunion last year, the old guy had become practically addicted to his computer. Few things in life were as entertaining as catching him doing screen time with another old military man and reliving the antics of their college years. Tough old dogs.

"I know how hard it is for you to let go of control," the General said.

Pot calling the kettle black. "I like things in order. There's a difference."

"Yes, there is." She could hear his smile.

Of all the grandchildren she was the most military in her thoroughness. If not for the need to rise before the sun and wear the most ghastly shades of khaki, she might have entertained a military career. Then again, there was no way she'd be the one doing the commanding at her age if she had.

"As I was saying," her grandfather continued, "I expect you to take it easy for at least a couple of days. Relax. Refresh your card playing skills."

She almost laughed at that one. There was no refreshing. She could annihilate the competition at cards since long before high school. That thoroughness allowed for an almost computer-like accounting of cards played. She didn't even need a color-coded system to keep track. "Don't you worry about my skill set."

"No. I suppose not." He chuckled. That sound was music to her ears. The gruff old man would always hide his tender heart behind his crusty Marine exterior. Whenever the shields came down was always extra special for any of his granddaughters. She was no exception. "I also thought it would be a good time for you to learn a bit more about—"

No, don't say it.

"Fishing." He'd said it.

At the ripe old age of six, she'd been bamboozled into doing something fun with her grandfather. Catching and handling slippery, slimy, wiggling, soon-to-be dead fish had not been fun. And she'd not been cajoled, coerced, or convinced to try it again since.

"We'll see." That response had worked about as well on her grandfather as it would on a six year old when her parents were actually saying not-likely-in-my-lifetime, but it was safer than outright digging her heels in the dirt.

"I bought you a fishing pole. It's pink."

"General," she bit back a laugh, "that hasn't been my favorite color since I was seven."

"Hm. Purple?"

"That's Poppy." Or maybe it was Callie. "Regardless, it doesn't matter if it's fourteen karat gold. I can run a successful art world fundraiser without learning to paint. I'm sure an auction at a fishing tournament will work the same way."

"We'll see."

Two words that made her cringe. When voiced by a retired US Marine Corps general, the words held a completely different meaning than when uttered by young parents. Already she was considering what outfit had she brought that would match a pink fishing pole.

Available at your favorite bookseller.

MEET CHRIS

USA TODAY Bestselling Author of more than a dozen contemporary novels, including the award-winning *Champagne Sisterhood*, Chris Keniston lives in suburban Dallas with her husband, two human children, and two canine children. Though she loves her puppies equally, she admits being especially attached to her German Shepherd rescue. After all, even dogs deserve a happily ever after.

More on Chris and her books can be found at
www.chriskeniston.com

Follow Chris on Facebook at ChrisKenistonAuthor
or on Twitter @ckenistonauthor

Questions? Comments?
I would love to hear from you.
You can reach me at chris@chriskeniston.com